Cassandra-Jamie

Cassandra-Jamie

❧ ❧ ❧

MILDRED AMES

Charles Scribner's Sons | New York

Library of Congress Cataloging in Publication Data
Ames, Mildred.   Cassandra—Jamie.
Summary: Once she decides to arrange her father's
marriage to the English teacher she adores,
Jamie begins to discover people are not always
as they seem to be on the surface.
[1. Teacher-student relationships—Fiction.
2. Fathers and daughters—Fiction.   3. Remarriage—Fiction]
I. Title.
PZ7.A5143Cas   1985   [Fic]   85-40297
ISBN 0-684-18472-9

Charles Scribner's Sons
Macmillan Publishing Company
866 Third Avenue, New York, NY 10022
Collier Macmillan Canada, Inc.

Printed in the United States of America

First Edition

3 5 7 9 11 13 15 17 19   F/C   20 18 16 14 12 10 8 6 4 2

To my dear friend,
Alice Warner Kuhns

Contents

❧ 1 ❧

Cassandra-Jamie

The new teacher wrote the words *Ms. Schuyler* on the chalkboard. "Before any of you have trouble with my name, I'll tell you right now that it's simply pronounced *Sky-ler*."

Jamie stared at the woman with the strange feeling that she already knew her yet couldn't place her.

"As many of you know, Ms. Doherty is on an indefinite medical leave so I'll be taking over her seventh grade English classes. What I'd like to do right now is go around the room and get acquainted as quickly as we can. Starting over here," she said, pointing to the side of the room opposite Jamie's, "give me your name and tell me briefly what you hope to get out of this class this year."

Jamie studied the teacher carefully. Short, straight, blond hair, worn behind her ears, looked as if she gave it little thought. Ms. Schuyler wore no makeup, but Jamie very much admired her tan, outdoorsy look. Even better, a wide smile, which she used often, made her seem like the kind of person you just knew would enjoy a good joke.

Why did she look so familiar? Jamie wondered. Could she have substituted in one of her other classes at some point?

Jamie was so caught up in puzzling over the woman that she was startled to suddenly discover it was her turn and the teacher was waiting for her to speak. She had quite forgotten what she was supposed to say. Oh, her name. "Jamie Cole," she said quickly.

Ms. Schuyler looked over the record where she'd been checking off names. "I don't see you listed. Oh, wait a minute—I have a Cassandra Cole." She stared questioningly at Jamie.

Jamie blushed. She hated to be the center of attention. "I prefer to use my middle name."

Ms. Schuyler flashed a bright smile that revealed a row of perfect teeth. "Then *Jamie* it shall be. Now, suppose you tell us what you hope to get out of English this semester."

Oh, dear. At the moment Jamie had no idea what she hoped to get out of this honors English class. She couldn't say she hoped to learn more about grammar, because that wouldn't be true. Conjugating verbs and diagraming sentences were the most boring pastimes she could imagine. But there *was* one thing she loved—the sound of beautiful words. She said, "I guess I'd like to learn more about what whole poems mean."

"In what way?" Ms. Schuyler asked.

"I mean, sometimes I only understand some of the lines

and phrases. I think I'd like some poems better if I knew their whole meaning."

Ms. Schuyler smiled. "I'm glad you mentioned poetry. I understand that you all had extensive grammar drilling last semester. I thought we'd go lighter on grammar this term and heavier on writing and reading. Naturally poetry will be an important part of our reading."

At that point the door to the room opened, and all eyes turned toward it. Gavin MacLaren, who should have been in his seat long ago, strode in and, with a businesslike gait, marched up to the teacher's desk. He was a thin, sandy-haired boy with an impertinence that tried many authority figures.

Uh-oh, Jamie thought. What was he up to now? Gavin was definitely not her favorite person. He lived close to her and spent far too much time wandering in and out of her house. He was such a show-off and such a pain. She couldn't figure out why Agnes, their housekeeper, put up with him.

When he reached Ms. Schuyler's side, Gavin clicked his heels together and, very militarylike, stood stiffly at attention, apparently waiting permission to speak.

Amusement glinted in Ms. Schuyler's eyes as she said, "Yes?"

"Gavin MacLaren, ma'am."

She stared at him curiously for a moment. Then the name obviously jogged her memory because she glanced at her list. "Oh, yes," she said and put a check mark on the paper. "You're very late."

"Yes, ma'am. Please allow me to apologize. I was unavoidably detained by—if you'll permit me—a call of nature. I know that's inexcusable. One should always time one's calls to occur between classes." His expression was so solemn and innocent that Jamie could tell Ms. Schuyler wasn't sure how to take him. Still, the teacher had to be aware that all the kids were sniggering.

"Please sit down," she said with a slight frown on her face.

Instead of doing that, Gavin said, "If I've given any offense, please accept my most sincere apology. I know that it is an honor to be allowed into this great edifice of learning, and I would consider it one of the bleak moments of my life if I have, in any way, offended anybody. I implore you to accept my apology." Poker-faced, he went on and on, apologizing and apologizing, until the whole class howled with laughter. Jamie knew what he was doing. He must have stayed up all night rehearsing that speech. He always led the way in taking apart a new teacher.

Ms. Schuyler waited him out. When he finally came to the end of his spiel, she said, "Are you quite finished?"

"With the call of nature?" Everyone howled again. "As a matter of fact, I am. You see, I was—"

"That's enough!" Ms. Schuyler's voice cut through the

4

laughter and stopped what promised to be a lengthy and probably graphic description of Gavin's nature call. "Go sit down, Gavin."

Gavin obligingly took his seat, still wearing an expression of angelic innocence.

"Now where was I?" Ms. Schuyler said. "Oh, yes, I was talking about the poetry we'll be reading this semester."

Somebody groaned.

"Was that a vote of confidence I just heard?" she asked.

Gavin said, "That was the moan of a man condemned to the guillotine."

Ms. Schuyler's eyes rested on him for a moment before she said, "I take it you're the class comic."

Gavin bowed his head in mock humility. "Modesty prohibits me from answering that question, ma'am." Again everyone laughed. Jamie wondered how he managed the dead-pan expression. That was really what broke people up.

Ms. Schuyler said, "As long as you like amusing an audience so much, Gavin, we'll do some dramatic readings. I'll see that you have a good meaty part to learn. Then you can earn applause in a more constructive way."

Jamie could tell from the look on Gavin's face that he knew he had gone one step too far. If he had any clever retorts this time, he kept them to himself.

"And so, back to poetry," Ms. Schuyler said.

Now everybody groaned.

"You mean you don't like poetry?" There was a look of mock horror on her face. When no one responded, she said, "Hey, you guys, poetry can be a lot of fun." She put her fingers on her forehead. "Let me think." After a moment she said, "All right, how about this one: 'Don't worry if your job is small,/And your rewards are few./Remember that the mighty oak,/Was once a nut like you.'" There were a few self-conscious sniggers. "Or how about this? 'There was a young lady of Lynn,/Who was so uncommonly thin/That when she essayed/To drink lemonade,/She slipped through the straw and fell in.'" She went on reciting short pieces of nonsense poetry that soon had the whole class chuckling.

Jamie had always loved nonsense poetry. Her favorite was Lewis Carroll's "Jabberwocky." For months she had driven everyone at home mad exclaiming, *O frabjous day! Callooh! Callay!* She felt that she just had to be Ms. Schuyler's most appreciative audience. And she had to marvel at how the teacher seemed to be in control of the class. Gavin had shaken her poise for a moment, but she had obviously recovered. Keeping the upper hand in a classroom could try even the most experienced teachers, and Ms. Schuyler looked too young to have been around that long. Perhaps, though, that was to her advantage. The class might feel that, because she was younger than most of their teachers, she would be more with it and, consequently, could understand them better. Then, too,

6

she had the poised, confident look of someone you might find on television—an anchorwoman, for example—rather than someone you'd find at Sheffield Heights Middle School. She was certainly quite a contrast to Ms. Doherty, who was about a hundred years older and about a hundred pounds heavier.

All through class Jamie kept mulling over why the woman looked so familiar. When the bell finally rang, Ms. Schuyler said, "Oh, yes—your assignment is to write your own definition of poetry in as few or as many words as you choose." There were more groans, but she only laughed good-naturedly.

Jamie deliberately dawdled while getting her books together, and her friend, Trudy Kirsch, said, "Come on, Jamie. Hurry up. I don't want to be late for gym."

Trudy was really Debbie Michaels's best friend, but they let Jamie make a third when it was convenient. Jamie felt that was only because their mothers encouraged them to do so. Since her mother had died, she knew she had become Poor Jamie to all her friends' mothers. Once she'd even overheard Trudy's mother say to Trudy and Debbie, "If you're going to the Saturday matinee, why don't you ask Poor Jamie to go with you?" Poor Jamie. How she hated to think of herself that way. Yet she knew very well that it was only because Debbie was not in the gifted program with them that Jamie and Trudy went to classes together.

Jamie said, "You go ahead, Trudy. I'll meet you there. I have to ask Ms. Schuyler something about the assignment."

Trudy grumbled but finally trundled off to the gym. Jamie picked up her books and shyly headed toward the desk where Ms. Schuyler now sat, poring over some papers. Jamie had to clear her throat to get the teacher's attention.

When Ms. Schuyler glanced up and saw Jamie, her eyes twinkled. "Well, Cassandra-Jamie Cole, what can I do for you?"

"I was wondering if maybe at some time you substituted in one of my classes in elementary school?"

Ms. Schuyler shook her head. "No, I've never taught in elementary school."

"Maybe last year in sixth grade then?"

"No." The teacher looked amused now.

"Then were you ever on television?"

Ms. Schuyler laughed now, a nice throaty laugh. "No, I've never been on television. What's this all about anyhow?"

Jamie hesitated, then said, "Well, it's just that I thought I'd met you someplace, but I can't remember where."

"I don't think so, Jamie. You see, my family and I have always lived in San Francisco, a good hundred miles from Sheffield Heights."

"Then maybe that's it. I've visited some of my relatives in San Francisco. Maybe I saw you there."

"How long ago was that?"

"About three years."

Ms. Schuyler laughed again. "Either you'd have to have a remarkable memory, or I'd have to have a remarkable face to stay with you that long."

"I guess I must be wrong, but you just look so familiar."

"Chalk it up to having a common face."

Jamie said quickly, "Oh, no. You certainly don't have that."

"Thank you—I think." She grinned at Jamie. "Now tell me something. Why does a girl with a first name like Cassandra want to be called by her middle name, Jamie?"

"Oh, Jamie isn't really my middle name. That's Jamison, my mother's maiden name."

"But Cassandra is such a beautiful name. It's straight out of Greek mythology."

Jamie was quiet for a moment. At length, she said, "Yes, I know."

"Then why Jamie and not Cassandra?"

"Well, you see, Cassandra was my mother's name. There's always been a Cassandra in our family. It's kind of a tradition. My father said it was confusing, having two Cassandras in the house, so my mother decided to call me Jamie. She said that when she was in college, all the girls

9

in the dorm used to call each other by their last names. They finally shortened hers to Jamie. She said she liked it, and when she wanted to give me a nickname, that was the first one she thought of. Then after she died, no one thought of going back to . . ." Jamie broke off. She hadn't intended saying any of this, but somehow the words had just rolled off her tongue.

After she died . . . After Jamie and her dad had gone through that long, horrible period of mourning, after she had no more tears to shed, no one had thought of calling her Cassandra now that there was only one of them in the house. Not even Jamie.

Jamie was aware that Ms. Schuyler's eyes were resting softly on her. "I see," Ms. Schuyler said, and Jamie had the feeling that she really *did* see. She said. "Jamie's a cute name, and if it feels good on you, I say, wear it."

"Thank you," Jamie said, then realized how inappropriate the words sounded.

Ms. Schuyler gave her a sweet smile. "Won't you be late for your next class?"

Jamie had been completely unaware that kids were already pouring into the room for Ms. Schuyler's next class. "Oh, yes, I guess I'd better run."

She scurried out and, on the way to gym, decided that Ms. Schuyler not only looked familiar, but she seemed like someone Jamie had known forever.

❧ 2 ❧

An Important Discovery

Jamie had lived in Sheffield Heights all her life. The town boasted a college, a lake, its own symphony orchestra, and an amphitheater for open-air performances on warm summer nights. The shops, filled with the arts and crafts of local artisans, were always described as "quaint." Jamie had never given the place much thought. Now, as she walked home from school, she wondered if someone like Ms. Schuyler, coming from a big city like San Francisco, would find it a hick town.

As she approached her house, she tried to see it through the teacher's eyes. It was a nice enough place, rambling and comfortable, but probably uninteresting if you compared it to one of the San Francisco Victorians. The house sat far back on a wide lawn, and behind it stretched four acres of land. Jamie especially loved the small patch of woods that was a part of their property. When she was lonely she spent time there talking to all the wildlife that she knew had just skittered away at her step. The sight of some elusive animal or insect always thrilled her and cheered her up.

Inside the house, Jamie found Agnes in the kitchen, chopping up onions for one of the casseroles she prepared for dinner almost every night. Agnes and her husband, Hector Bagby, had worked for the Coles even before Jamie's mother's death. Hector said his health wouldn't allow him to work indoors, so he did the gardening and minor repairs while Agnes kept up the house, cooked, and looked after Jamie. She and Hector lived on the property in what was once a guest house.

As Jamie entered the kitchen, Agnes glanced up, tears spilling down her cheeks. Jamie's stomach tightened. "You're crying."

Agnes wiped away the tears with the back of a hand. "It's these doggone onions. Talk about Los Angeles smog—these fumes are so strong I could get arrested for polluting the environment."

Agnes was a native of Los Angeles. Jamie, a note of fear in her voice, said, "You're not thinking of going back there, are you, Agnes?"

"No, *ma'am.* I'll take the onions over L.A. any day."

Jamie relaxed. "What are you making?"

"Carmelita's Special."

"Is that the stuff with hamburger, corn chips, and beans?"

"It has hamburger, corn chips, and beans, but it is not stuff."

"Last week you said it was José's Special."

"Last week we didn't have a green pepper in the house. This week we do, and that makes it Carmelita's Special."

Agnes wasn't a fancy cook, yet her food always tasted good, and her invented names made it sound more interesting than it was. She was ancient, Jamie thought, almost fifty, yet she never seemed to be still a minute.

Jamie dumped her books on a kitchen chair, draped her jacket over the back of it, took a glass from the cupboard, opened the refrigerator, and helped herself to some milk. As Agnes browned hamburger and onions in a large cast-iron pan, Jamie sat down at the kitchen table for her usual after-school chat.

Agnes said, as she always did, "So how was your day?"

And, as always, Jamie said, "Okay." Then she realized that this day was just a little more interesting than "okay," so she added, "I have a new teacher for English. And you know something, Agnes, I just felt so sure I knew her from someplace, but she says no."

Above the sizzle of hamburger, Agnes said, "Lots of people look familiar. It's got something to do with physical types."

"No, it wasn't like that. It was much more. I mean, I just felt as though I knew how she'd sound before she even opened her mouth. As though I'd known her forever and ever."

"So maybe she's somebody you knew in a former life."

Agnes, an authority on the subject, believed very strongly in reincarnation. So did Jamie. "You know, Agnes, I never thought of that. Maybe that's what it is. And if it is, I wonder what we were to each other then. I mean, how could I remember her without her remembering me?"

Agnes frowned down into the hamburger as she vigorously stirred it. "Happens that way sometimes. Could be she was your teacher in another life. Over the years teachers have so many pupils they're apt to forget a few of them."

Jamie sipped her milk and thought about it. Would there have been the same age difference between them in a previous life? She thought so. Maybe, as Agnes suggested, Ms. Schuyler had been her beloved teacher. Or she could have even been someone closer, like an older sister. Jamie drained her glass, got up, put it in the dishwasher, and scooped up her books and jacket from the kitchen chair. "I'll have to give it some serious thought."

"You do that," Agnes said, but her attention was on the makings for Carmelita's Special. "Maybe you'll figure it out."

Sometimes Jamie wasn't sure Agnes was taking her seriously. Today was one of those times.

"By the way," Agnes said, "your daddy won't be here for dinner tonight. He has an engagement."

Jamie scowled. "Who with?"

"I believe it's with that Dennis woman."

"Again?" Jamie didn't bother to hide her annoyance.

"Jamie, it's only natural for a grown man to want the company of a woman once in a while. You gotta get used to the idea."

"He was out with her three times last week. Today's only Monday. What's he doing—working up to every night?"

"So what if he does?"

"So I don't have to like it, do I?" Before Agnes could answer, Jamie stomped off to her room, then threw her books onto the desk and herself onto the bed. She stared up at the ceiling.

She wasn't quite sure how she felt about Sylvia Dennis because she'd never even met her. As far as she knew, this was the first time since her mother's death three years ago that her father had dated anyone, and she didn't like the idea. Outside of that, she really had nothing against the woman. Well, with the possible exception of her being divorced. Jamie didn't much care for the invention of divorce. Sylvia Dennis had what sounded like an interesting job, though. She was a buyer for something called the Fine Dress Salon at I. Magnin.

To take her mind away from her father and his date,

15

Jamie concentrated on why Ms. Schuyler looked so famil-iar. She knew she would have to think hard, but she was certain that, when she found the answer, it would have some great importance in her life.

Sisters. An interesting thought. In ancient Egypt? In Elizabethan times? Jamie's imagination placed them both in some medieval castle, members of the nobility, sitting in a great chamber where Ms. Schuyler was showing Jamie, her younger sister, how to do intricate needlework. The two of them were giggling over some shared secret as the other ladies of the court glared at them, jealous of their intimacy, jealous of all the fun they had together. Jamie smiled at the thought. She brought the image of the teacher again to mind until she could see her very clearly—the tan, smiling face; the short, blond hair.

Jamie got up and took herself back to the kitchen where Agnes was now spooning ingredients for Carmelita's Special into an earthenware casserole. Jamie said, "I sure wish I'd inherited my mother's blond hair."

Agnes gave her a cursory glance. "Nothing wrong with brown hair. Besides, most blonds start turning dark by the time they're your age anyhow. After that, it all comes out of a bottle."

"Not my mother's."

"Oh, yes, your mother's, too."

"Really, Agnes?"

"Yes, really."

Jamie fell silent for a moment. "Now that you mention it, I do remember her doing something to her hair. I asked her about it once, and she said she was putting sunlight in it."

Agnes chuckled. "Sunlight's the name of the brand she used." She went on layering the ingredients for her casserole. "Nothing wrong with giving nature a helping hand, I always say."

Jamie slumped into a kitchen chair. "I suppose I could always bleach mine."

Agnes stopped what she was doing and jabbed her spoon in Jamie's face. "Now don't you go getting any ideas. Nature didn't mean for you to be a blond. You got your daddy's black eyes and olive complexion. You'd look like a trollop."

If there was one thing Agnes really hated, Jamie knew, it was anyone who looked like a trollop. She shrugged and dropped the subject. "I guess I'd better start my homework," she said and got up.

"Now, *that's* a good idea."

Jamie trotted back to her room. First, she worked on her math assignment. When she finished, she started thinking about what Ms. Schuyler had asked for—a definition of poetry. Her own definition.

Poetry. Could anyone define poetry? What was it anyhow? If anything, it was feelings more than words. Or was it only words that evoked feelings? She was never sure of what all the lines of most poems meant, but she loved the sound of the words.

Last Christmas her grandmother had sent her an anthology of poetry. At first she'd thought it was a dumb gift, but after a while she'd made some wonderful discoveries in it. She particularly liked some of the lines from Emily Dickinson. Like "Bring me the sunset in a cup." How beautiful to think of a cup full of sunset. And no matter what Agnes said, she would always believe that her mother had put sunlight in her hair. That was poetry too: seeing and remembering what was beautiful.

Jamie got up and went over to her dresser, where she picked up a photograph of her mother and stared at it intently. Then she marched back to the kitchen and held it up to Agnes. "Agnes, you said this wasn't a good likeness of my mother."

Agnes studied the picture for a moment. "No, it's not. She was better-looking."

Jamie nodded slowly, deliberately. "Now I know."

"Now you know what?"

"Now I know who my new English teacher reminds me of. She looks an awful lot like my mother." The question that had nagged Jamie ever since she'd met Ms. Schuyler faded, and a wonderful serenity replaced it.

But Agnes looked disturbed.

✤ 3 ✤

The Sunset in a Cup

More than a week had passed since Ms. Schuyler had taken over Jamie's English class. During that time Jamie learned, from one source or another, a few interesting facts about her. Ms. Schuyler had put in two years at Yale University, then completed her education in a college closer to San Francisco, her home. After graduation, she'd spent a year tramping about Europe. Jamie tucked away all these precious bits of information in a special compartment of her mind labeled *Ms. Schuyler*.

Jamie sat in class dreaming as Ms. Schuyler read aloud the definitions of poetry the students had turned in as their first assignment. Instead of poetry, Jamie was thinking about how, as the days went by, the teacher reminded her more and more of her mother. Oh, not that Ms. Schuyler's features were the same. The resemblance was more in mannerisms: the way she held her head, the way her fingers touched her forehead when she puzzled over some forgotten bit of information. And her hair was

19

exactly the same shade of blond, although Jamie's mother had worn hers longer.

As the teacher read, Jamie paid scant attention until her ear sensed a change in Ms. Schuyler's tone as she said. "How do you feel about this one, class?" Then she quoted from the paper, " 'If it's hard to read, it's poetry. If it sounds like it's been written by somebody with a belly-ache, it's poetry. I predict this form will never last.' "

When the kids started to laugh, Jamie felt the anger rise within her. She knew very well who had written those words and so did the whole class. Jamie decided that she really hated Gavin MacLaren. She glanced across the room to see him taking mock bows from his seat, like a performer acknowledging applause.

When the laughter died, Ms. Schuyler said, "I asked how you felt about that definition of poetry—anybody?"

Jamie's hand shot up.

"Yes, Jamie?"

"I feel . . . I think it's dumb. And I think that Ga—, I mean, the writer is the kind of person that nobody should pay any attention to because he," she corrected herself quickly, "or she, will say any dumb thing for a laugh." Out of the corner of her eye she could see Gavin making a face at her.

Ms. Schuyler said, "Well, if you're right, Jamie, if our writer is trying only for laughs—which, you'll have to admit, he *did* get—then perhaps he *has* communicated successfully. After all, isn't that what writing is all about—trying to draw a specific response from a reader?"

Jamie felt confused. She'd tried to protect Ms. Schuyler from Gavin, and now the teacher was saying that what Gavin had written was fine. Jamie glanced quickly his way to see his tongue shoot out at her.

"On the other hand," Ms. Schuyler said, "if the writer is serious and really believes that poetry is that bad, then I'll just have to work hard at trying to change his mind before the term is over."

Jamie saw Gavin give his I-dare-you-to-try-it shrug.

Ms. Schuyler either didn't see him, or she ignored him. "Let's continue," she said and started to read from one of the other papers. " 'Poetry is not what you see but what you don't see. It is the hidden side of the moon, the back of your head, the naked sun, your soul. And only people with laser-beam eyes can take it all in and show you what you could never see by yourself.' "

There was a moment of silence, and Jamie felt her face go all hot. She had felt so proud of herself when she'd completed that assignment. Now the words read in class embarrassed her. She felt as if everyone could see into her mind and heart. Then she remembered with relief that only Ms. Schuyler knew she had written the piece.

Ms. Schuyler finally said, "What do you think of that definition, class?"

Gavin was the only one to raise his hand. When she

nodded for him to speak, he stood up and exaggeratedly arranged his body in an at-attention position, then he said very solemnly, "I think this writer will say any dumb thing for a laugh."

Jamie's mouth dropped open. Could he possibly have known that she had written the words? Instead of laughter, this time his words were met with an uneasy silence.

Ms. Schuyler said, "Gavin, the most important asset for a comic is timing. At the moment, yours happens to be way off."

Gavin shrugged, obviously trying to feign indifference, and sat down.

I really, really hate him, Jamie thought. He must have guessed that the last piece was hers. He was always saying that she talked like some character in a book rather than like a real person. To Jamie's relief, the buzzer sounded. Before she could get to her feet to join Trudy Kirsch and head for their next class, Ms. Schuyler said, "Jamie, will you stay a few minutes, please?"

Jamie motioned for Trudy to go ahead. As everyone filed out, the teacher joined Jamie at her desk. Jamie kept wondering what she had done wrong. Was she out of line, putting down Gavin the way she had? To her relief, Ms. Schuyler smiled at her and said, "In spite of our class comic, that was a remarkable piece of work you turned in. Do you realize that, Cassandra-Jamie?"

All Jamie realized was that Ms. Schuyler had just handed her the sunset in a cup.

Jamie walked slowly, regally, in the wooded area behind her house. Not even a squirrel was visible this day, this strange and indescribable day. She paused, lifted her head toward the sky, and thrust out her arms theatrically. "I, Cassandra," she said, "have the gift of prophecy. It is a gift not to be taken lightly." Then she dropped her hands to her sides and sighed deeply. As she stood there the shadows seemed to deepen, and she hugged herself against the chill of the late afternoon.

A beam from the low sun found its way through the trees and cast an eerie glow on the path just ahead of her. An indescribably lovely, mysterious glow. She moved forward slowly and held out her arms, reaching toward it until her hands were covered with light. Then she turned up her palms and stared down as the rosy rays of the sun washed over them. *The sunset in a cup.* The cup of her hands. Oh, she would long remember the wonder, the beauty of this moment. The indescribable, exquisite beauty of this moment, this day. Now she stood within the circle of light, letting it spill over her. Blood of the gods, christening her anew, giving her magical powers.

"I, Cassandra," she said, "have the gift of prophecy. O, hear me, all you woodland creatures, for I have the wis-

dom of sages. From this day forth, I am reborn." A god-
dess now, she turned and walked, in a dream, along the
path that led to her house. The dying sun painted the
world in shades of purple, mauve, and rose. Indescribably beautiful, yet achingly sad. At her back door, she
gave another sigh, one that divested her of all her royal
raiment. Once again Jamie, she went inside.

The enchantment completely fled when she saw Agnes
setting the table in the kitchen. On nights when her father
took a client to dinner or was out of town on business, she
ate there with Agnes and Hector. She hadn't realized that
this was to be one of those nights.

"I suppose Daddy's having dinner with that woman
again," Jamie said.

"I didn't ask," Agnes said, "but I got the impression it
was business."

That made Jamie feel a little better. Her father was a
corporate lawyer, and although she felt that business
trips and dinners took up too much of his time, they were
still better than the thought of his dining with Sylvia
Dennis.

In the warmth of the kitchen, she took off her jacket
and slung it over a shoulder. She could smell one of
Agnes's casseroles baking in the oven, but she had more
important things than food on her mind. Until that moment, she had kept the wonder of her talk with Ms.

Schuyler to herself. Now that she'd had time to absorb it, she felt the need to share it with someone. "You know something, Agnes?"

Agnes, who was busy taking dishes from the cupboard, gave a perfunctory, "What?"

"Today Ms. Schuyler said that one of the assignments I did for her was remarkable."

"What assignment was that?"

"She asked us to write our own definition of poetry. She said that, in all her years of teaching, mine was the best she'd ever gotten from any of her pupils."

"Well, now, that was nice."

"Yes. And you know what else? She said some people are gifted with extraordinary sensitivity—extraordinary, Agnes—and she said I might just be one of them, and that maybe I might become a poet or an author or something like that."

"Sensitivity, eh? Well, I'd say she was right about that. I always told you that you get your feelings hurt too easily."

Jamie paid no attention to her. "And something else, Agnes. I found out what her first name is. I overheard one of the teachers call her Alex. Then when I was going into English the other day, one of the teachers stopped me outside the room and asked me if I'd take an envelope to Ms. Schuyler. Of course I said yes, and when I took it, I noticed that the name typed outside was Alexandra Schuyler. Isn't that a great name? Alexandra. It sounds so strong and elegant."

Agnes muttered some indistinguishable answer as she went about setting the table.

Jamie, off in a world of her own, said, "Once in a while Ms. Schuyler tells us a little about the year she spent in Europe. Yesterday she mentioned the palace at Versailles. She says it's indescribably beautiful."

Agnes said good-naturedly, "Ms. Schuyler, Ms. Schuyler, that's all you talk about anymore. Come on, now. Put your jacket in your room and wash up. Dinner will be ready in a few minutes, and if you're not here before Hector, you just might go indescribably hungry."

Before Jamie could leave, the back door opened and in walked Gavin MacLaren, a plastic two-cup measuring cup in his hands. It seemed to Jamie that he was always at her house, either borrowing or paying back sugar.

"What is it, Gavin?" Agnes asked. "You can't need sugar again this soon."

With an air of mock indignation, Gavin said, "You wrong me, Lady Agnes. I'm good for every granule I borrow." He held up the plastic cup. "Look you at this silver chalice. Behold, it is full to the brim with a substance that could never compare to the sweetness of your sweet smile."

26

Jamie was annoyed to see Agnes flash Gavin one of her sweet smiles as she said, "You're going to rot your teeth with all that candy you make. Fudge, is it?"

"Up to now it's mostly been kitchen failures, but I'll perfect the art yet."

"I bet you don't let on to your mom that you make so much sweet stuff."

"The drill sergeant? No, you're right. There are many things Dad and I don't tell her." He shook his head solemnly. "Concern for her health, you see. We have to watch her blood pressure."

Agnes said, "I didn't know she had high blood pressure."

"She doesn't, but she would if we let her get excited. And, believe me, it doesn't take much."

"Well, all I can say is it's a good thing your dad is a dentist."

"Yeah. He's got a good practice. I eat plenty of candy, and he gets lots of practice on me."

"Oh, very funny," Jamie said and rolled her eyes. "Gavin, you are indescribably boorish."

For the first time Gavin glanced her way. He shrugged. "Anything for a laugh, I always say."

She knew he was referring to what she'd said about him in class. "I know what you always say, and I'd just as soon not hear it. And I think you should keep your mouth shut

27

in English. Ms. Schuyler is a beautiful person, and she doesn't need your dumb jokes."

"If I have to keep my mouth shut in English, I suppose I can always talk Spanish."

Jamie gave a gasp of disgust and turned away from him. Agnes said, "I wish you two could stop your squabbling." She pointed to the neat row of canisters on the counter. "Gavin, you know where the sugar goes."

As Gavin put the sugar in the container, he said, "Man, something sure smells good in here."

Uh-oh, Jamie thought. Here it comes.

Agnes said, "That's Oriental Chicken Supreme."

"Is that the dish with water chestnuts and mushrooms and all that good stuff in it?" Gavin asked.

"The very same, complete with fortune cookies."

Gavin exclaimed, "Oh, man, that's a dish I really love."

Agnes grinned. "Does that mean you're not having anything you like at home tonight?"

"Oh, I wouldn't go so far as to say that. The drill sergeant had to go to a PTA meeting, so my sister and I get to eat our very favorite TV dinners. I can even have Chinese if I want. We've got one called Sub Gum Yuk. Of course, we don't have fortune cookies. What's a Chinese dinner without a fortune cookie? I always say."

"I get the message," Agnes said.

Sure you do, Jamie thought. She couldn't imagine why Agnes was such a pushover for Gavin.

Agnes said, "Call your house, Gavin. Tell your sister and your dad that you'll be eating here."

Jamie opened her mouth to say, *I'm not hungry so I think I'll skip dinner tonight.* Then the tantalizing sight and aroma of Agnes's casserole as it came from the oven made her realize that she was absolutely famished. The only thing she felt like skipping was her fortune cookie. She could already guess what it would say: *Some people put food ahead of principles.*

❧ 4 ❧

Gavin MacLaren

All through dinner Jamie felt sullen as Gavin chattered on and on, at one point mimicking characters from old movies he'd seen, all of which seemed to amuse Agnes and Hector. But not Jamie. She was too annoyed with Gavin to appreciate his imitations even when they were good.

Hector, a plump, easygoing man, about half a head shorter than Agnes, chuckled away at Gavin's antics. "You just might wind up in the movies one of these days," he said. "Make themselves a bundle, those comedian fellas."

Hector was very interested in making bundles. Jamie knew that if it wasn't for Agnes he would have lost their every cent in the stock market. In fact, he had just about done that when Agnes put her foot down. Enough was enough. From that day on, Agnes had handled their money. Hector could buy and sell only on paper. He watched the stock market returns on public television every day. Then before the market closed he jotted down his choices. He kept his list in a folder he called his portfolio.

Jamie thought the whole thing looked like an indecipherable jumble of figures, but Hector insisted he knew exactly what he was doing and was well ahead of the game, and if only Agnes wasn't so tight with money, they could both be on easy street. "Yessir," he said again to Gavin, "a good stand-up comedian can sure make a bundle. You ought to think about that for a career."

"Actually, I *have* been thinking very seriously about a career lately. I want something with good hours, lots of money, and not much work," Gavin said.

Hector shook his fork at him. "Then you better think about what I just said, boy."

"Not a bad idea, but I was thinking of something more like master criminal," Gavin said, straight-faced.

For a moment Jamie thought Hector was taking Gavin seriously. Then he gave a tolerant smile and shook his head.

Agnes said, "You be careful with what you say, Gavin. Someday somebody's going to believe you, and you'll be sorry."

Jamie piped up with, "And someday he's going to say something that gets him kicked out of school."

"Oh, yeah?" Gavin said. "And who's going to do it— your beautiful person, Ms. Schuyler?"

"She might," Jamie said.

"Oh, no, she won't. You know why?"

"Why?"

31

"Because the woman she's staying with is Darlene Walker, and Darlene Walker just happens to work in my mother's travel agency, and Schuyler knows it. She wouldn't do anything to make her friend lose her job."

"Now, Gavin MacLaren, you stop talking like that or you *will* sound like a master criminal," Agnes chided. "Besides, you're just dreaming. From what I know of your mom, she'd be mighty apt to agree with your teacher."

Gavin looked sober for a moment. Then he smiled sheepishly. "Lady Agnes, I hate to admit it, but you are one-hundred-percent right. The drill sergeant would be the first to agree with her."

Jamie had never seen Gavin that subdued before. She'd have to ask Agnes about Gavin's mother when he was not around. Right now though, she was more interested in the information Gavin had given her. Earlier she had looked in vain for Ms. Schuyler's name in the phone book. Then she'd called information, but there was no listing for her. Now Jamie understood why. The phone would naturally be under the name Walker.

After Gavin left, she immediately took out the phone book and riffled through until she found a listing for a D. Walker at 1325 Conestoga Drive. She wrote down the phone number and the address and tucked them carefully away in her desk for future reference. Then she went out to the kitchen where she found Agnes alone and putting dishes in the dishwasher. She didn't have to ask where Hector was. He always disappeared immediately after dinner to watch television in the cottage where he and Agnes lived. Agnes stayed on until Jamie's father returned.

"You finished your homework?" Agnes asked.

"Almost. I've got a little more to do, but I wanted to ask you something about Gavin first."

"Oh? What's that?"

"Well, he kind of looked funny when you were talking about his mother. I wondered what that was all about."

Agnes stopped what she was doing and turned to face Jamie. "You know, Jamie, sometimes you're too hard on poor Gavin."

Poor Gavin. The words startled Jamie. Too often she'd heard herself referred to as Poor Jamie. "Why are you calling him *poor* Gavin?"

"Because I feel sorry for him, living with that mother of his. From what I hear from Mrs. Woods, their housekeeper, she's always on him about something. Worse than that, she keeps telling him that it's his fault that she gave up her acting career."

"I didn't know she had an acting career."

"Well, to tell you the truth, I don't think it was that big a deal. I guess she'd had a couple of small parts in movies before she married Dr. MacLaren. Then when Gavin's sister Caroline came along, she quit to stay home and raise her baby. I understand she decided to go back to work

33

when Caroline was old enough for school. She signed up with her agent again. Then when he got her a part in some soap opera, she discovered she was pregnant with Gavin. Now she says it's too late for the career she wanted. And all because of him."

"But why should she blame Gavin for that?"

"She shouldn't. The fact is, it's not doing him any good, burdening him with all that guilt. Some women just enjoy being martyrs, and I suspect she's one of them."

"Daddy says her travel agency is really successful."

"I know, and maybe she should be thanking Gavin for that. Her acting career might not have panned out as good. Well, anyhow, she's gone a lot, trotting all over the globe. I guess he gets a breather then." Agnes went back to loading the dishwasher as if she was through with the conversation.

But Jamie wasn't. "Is that why you're so nice to him? Because you feel sorry for him?"

"Partly. Behind all his wild antics, I can feel a lot of hurt. But I like Gavin, too. He's a bright kid. And as much as he tries to hide it, inside he's a real decent human being."

Jamie and Gavin were both in the mentally gifted program, so they saw a great deal of each other. If there was a decent human being inside Gavin, Jamie had yet to find him. "You sure could have fooled me," she said.

"Now, miss, don't act smart. Gavin doesn't get much

kindness and love at home. You can at least act civil to him."

"Civil, okay. But that's all."

"That's all I'm asking."

Jamie was tired of talking about Gavin. Agnes just wasn't a kid, that's all. If she had been, she'd have seen Gavin's true nature, which was anything but decent. To change the subject, she said, "Agnes, do you believe in destiny?"

Agnes stopped short. "What's that got to do with anything?"

Jamie perched on a kitchen chair, settling in for a long chat. "Well, nothing, I guess. I just happened to think of it, and I wondered how *you* felt."

Agnes shrugged. "Never gave it much thought. Can't say I believe in it or I don't."

"I mean, do you think people are destined to meet each other and it just couldn't be any other way?"

"Of course it could be some other way. I remember when I met Hector. Hector wanted to play pool that night and his buddy wanted to bowl, so they tossed a coin. Bowling won. And I just happened to go bowling that night with my girlfriend. If the coin had come up the other way, Hector would never have been a part of my life."

"But that's just it, Agnes. The coin came up that way because you were destined to meet Hector."

Agnes rolled her eyes heavenward. "If somebody up there is messing with coin tosses, all I've got to say is He could have picked a rich man to send to the bowling alley that night."

"But then you wouldn't have met Hector."

"If I lost Hector right now, I'd miss him. But if I hadn't met him in the first place, I couldn't miss him, could I? I'd be perfectly dumb and happy with a rich man on my arm."

"But, Agnes, if you hadn't met Hector, you would never have known me."

Agnes stopped her work to come over and give Jamie a quick hug. "You're absolutely right. If I'd married a rich man, I wouldn't have had to work, and if I didn't have to work, I'd never have met you. And that would have been a sad situation. Thought there for a minute I might send Hector back, but I guess I'd better keep him after all."

Jamie grinned. Hector and Agnes might bicker over little things from time to time, but Jamie had no doubt that they loved each other. "I truly believe in destiny, Agnes. I think there is some great power that knows your needs, even when you don't, and does whatever is necessary to fill them. And if bad things happen, it's only because something else good is coming up. I truly, truly believe that."

Agnes patted Jamie's hand. "It never hurts to think positive."

When Jamie returned to her room to finish her home-work, she smiled to herself, happy that the great power had chosen Ms. Schuyler to be a part of *her* destiny.

The following afternoon, when Gavin came over for his usual loan of sugar, Agnes was in the living room, vac-uuming. Jamie was in the kitchen alone, drinking milk and eating a handful of the jelly beans Agnes always kept in an antique candy jar on the table. "Don't you ever think of knocking?" she said to Gavin.

He reopened the door, reached around to the outside, and gave two smart knocks. "Who's there?" he said, then answered himself in a deep voice. "Dwayne." "Dwayne who?" he asked. The deep voice answered, "Dwayne is leaking in dwoof."

Jamie gave him her most bored-sounding sigh, then watched him head for the table, put down his cup, lift the lid of the candy jar, and help himself to a scoop of jelly beans.

"Why don't you have some jelly beans?" she said sarcastically.

"Good idea," he said and took a second scoop.

Jamie snatched his cup off the table and marched over to the canister. As she began filling the cup with sugar, one of the jelly beans she held in her hand, an orange one, dropped into the cup. She was going to fish it out, then decided that Gavin was only going to make candy so the

37

jelly bean would make no difference. She continued filling the cup, then took it back to him. "Doesn't anybody in your house *ever* buy sugar?"

"My father's a dentist, remember? He had to take an oath in dental college." Gavin put one hand over his heart and raised the other. " 'I do solemnly swear that not one grain of sugar shall cross the threshold of my house or find its way into the mouths of any of my children.' All dentists have to take it. They won't let them practice until they do. Why, Mrs. Woods has to sneak sugar from her own house just so I can pay you back."

For a moment Jamie almost believed him. Then she remembered that this was Gavin. "Can't you ever be serious about anything?"

He was too busy to answer her. He was tossing one jelly bean at a time straight up into the air and, as it came down, catching it in his mouth. When he missed one and it went rolling across the floor, he said, "Whoops. That's one for your side."

Jamie, frowning, placed the filled cup on the table. "There's your sugar." Then she gave him a haughty glare and said, "Now, if you'll excuse me, I have other things to do." She turned on her heel and, without even glancing back, strode out of the room. With Agnes busy, Gavin would have no excuse to hang around.

In her bedroom, she sat down and began her homework. A little later Agnes peeked in and said, "Jamie, I forgot to tell you, your daddy wants to take you out to dinner tonight."

"Oh, super," Jamie said. She loved nothing better than having dinner in some nice restaurant with candlelight and great big fancy menus and her father sitting across from her, making her feel so grown up.

Agnes said, "He wants you to meet Sylvia Dennis."

Oh. Jamie had to marvel at how a few simple words, a few indescribably simple words, could ruin a beautiful, beautiful evening.

❧ 5 ❧

Things Are Not Always
What They Seem

In Jamie's memory, her mother's face and figure were slowly altering to more and more resemble those of Ms. Schuyler. Tonight, as Jamie studied Sylvia Dennis across a table at Chez Maurice, her favorite restaurant, she couldn't help comparing Sylvia with the teacher.

Sylvia, as she'd asked Jamie to call her, was dark whereas Ms. Schuyler was fair. They were both slender, but Sylvia was taller and looked like something right out of a fashion magazine, handsome and hungry. She was probably vain and interested in nothing but herself, Jamie decided. She much preferred Ms. Schuyler's outdoorsy look.

All the girls she knew said her father was sexy-looking. Jamie couldn't see it. To her, he looked like a father. As Agnes said, he and Jamie both had the same dark eyes and hair, but he had a touch of gray at the temples. And he was starting to worry about whether he was getting a paunch. Definitely like a father.

They had all had lobster for dinner. If Sylvia was trying to maintain a model-thin figure, Jamie thought, no one would ever know it. Except that she'd skipped dessert, she'd eaten with as much enjoyment as Jamie herself, right down to the fattening sourdough bread.

Now, as Jamie finished her ice cream, Sylvia sighed contentedly and said, "Wonderful dinner, Rick. It's been ages since I've had lobster. It was delicious." As the waiter served coffee, she lit a cigarette. "Bad habit. I wish I could break it."

"I suppose it's hard to stop," Richard Cole said.

"Oh, no. Stopping is easy. I've done it thousands of times." When he smiled, she added, "Mark Twain, I think."

Jamie didn't smile. She would have bet anything that Ms. Schuyler didn't smoke. Sylvia would surely get lung cancer or that other awful disease that people who smoked came down with. What was her father thinking of, dating a woman who was destined to die an early death? Of course, her mother hadn't smoked, but she'd been born with the heart problem that had killed her.

Jamie, trying to sound as if she were making a casual remark, said, "My dad doesn't smoke at all. Neither did my mother."

Jamie could feel Sylvia's eyes resting on her strangely. Cautiously, perhaps? "I know," Sylvia said.

What did that mean? Naturally Sylvia knew that Jamie's father didn't smoke. Did she also know about her mother? And, if so, Jamie thought, her father must have told her. But why would they be talking about something like that?

Sylvia said, "Your father tells me you're in a gifted program. He must be very proud of you."

"You bet I am," her dad said.

"Do you enjoy the work?" Sylvia asked Jamie.

Jamie gave the answer she felt was expected of her. "Yes, because it's more challenging." That's what people were always saying anyhow. In truth, Jamie had been in the program so long she didn't know whether it was more demanding than a regular program or not. The work was there to do, and she simply did it. Like Agnes with the idea of destiny, Jamie never gave it much thought one way or the other.

"School was always hard for me," Sylvia said, "so I admire brainy people."

"It couldn't have been that hard, or you'd have never made it into college," Jamie's father said.

"I only lasted three years."

Jamie said, "My mother graduated."

Her father added quickly, "She always said it was quite a struggle for her, too."

Maybe so, Jamie thought, but she didn't quit after three years. Jamie was proud of the fact that her mother was a Vassar graduate. She planned to become one herself. Agnes always said that Vassar women were independent types. They went out into the community and did what had to be done, which had certainly been true of Jamie's mother. She'd done all kinds of volunteer work after Jamie was old enough to go to school. Jamie said to Sylvia, "Do you have any children?"

She couldn't quite read the expression on the woman's face. "No, I don't," Sylvia said. "I live alone in the Bristol Arms. Do you know where that is?"

To Jamie's surprise, she did. "Yes, on Broad Boulevard. One of the kids who used to be in my class lived there." Jamie had liked Lisa Chan and had visited her at the Bristol Arms once, a somewhat run-down building. Lisa said her parents didn't mind the place because her father was on temporary assignment, and they would soon return to their comfortable home in Milwaukee. Jamie, if she had bothered to think about it, would have pictured Sylvia living in some new, expensive, and very modern condominium.

"You'll have to come see my apartment sometime," Sylvia said to Jamie.

Fat chance, Jamie thought. She said, "That would be nice." A stream of Sylvia's killer smoke wafted her way. She deliberately made a great show of fanning the air.

Sylvia looked chastened. "Oh, sorry." She stubbed out her cigarette in the ashtray. "I wish I could quit."

"Let's get the bill and get out of here," Jamie's father said.

Jamie was only too willing.

43

* * *

The following day in English class, as Ms. Schuyler had different students read aloud from Alfred Tennyson's *Idylls of the King*, Jamie's mind wandered. Why couldn't her father have driven Sylvia home first instead of dropping Jamie off, then disappearing with Sylvia for what seemed like ages? She and Agnes were watching television when he finally walked in. Agnes had a few things to tell him about the household, then she excused herself.

Jamie came right to the point. "How come you didn't drive Sylvia home first? You would have saved a trip."

Without answering, he walked over and switched off the television set.

"Why'd you do that?" Jamie demanded.

"Because I want to talk to you."

Her father was seldom stern with her, but she could tell there was something serious on his mind now. He settled himself in a chair near the sofa where she was sitting and leaned forward. "I took you home first because it's a school night and you said you had homework to do."

"But it wouldn't have taken that long to take her home."

"Jamie, I wanted to visit with Sylvia."

"I don't see why."

She could see a look of annoyance cross his face. "You don't have to see why, but the fact is I happen to enjoy her company. Is that so hard to understand?"

Jamie wanted to say yes, but she merely shrugged.

44

"Jamie, I don't think you behaved very well this evening."

Jamie bristled. "I don't know what you mean."

"I think you do. In the first place, I don't think it was very nice of you to point out that your mother never smoked. You sounded as if you were making comparisons and condemning Sylvia."

"I was. Smoking is a—a vile habit."

A deep frown formed on her father's face. "For your information, your mother *did* smoke when we got married. She gave it up soon afterward because the doctor told her it wasn't doing her heart condition any good. And she didn't have an easy time stopping either. She finally had to go to one of those centers that help people quit."

Jamie thought she'd known everything there was to know about her mother, yet she hadn't known that. "Well, at least *she* stopped."

"Now listen to me, Jamie. Whether or not Sylvia smokes is none of your business."

Jamie gave her I-couldn't-care-less shrug.

Her father went on, "From now on, I don't want you comparing Sylvia with your mother the way you did tonight. And don't pretend you don't know what I'm talking about. It's very hurtful to be put down that way."

"I don't see why I can't talk about my mother if I want to."

"No one is stopping you from talking about your

45

mother. Just don't make comparisons. Sylvia is an entirely different person. There is no reason why she should be like your mother."

"I didn't realize I was making comparisons."

"I think you did."

Jamie changed the subject. "How long was she married?"

"Sylvia? Oh, about ten years, I think."

"I bet she's selfish."

"Selfish! Why would you think a thing like that when you hardly know her?"

"Because she doesn't have any kids. People who don't want kids are always selfish."

Her father gasped with disbelief. "Jamie, don't be so quick to judge. You've spent less than a couple of hours with the woman, and you think you know all about her."

"Sometimes you can tell a lot about a person from first impressions," Jamie said.

"That's seldom the case, Jamie. The fact is, Sylvia *did* have a child—a little boy. He was killed in a car accident when he was only five years old. It was a terrible tragedy."

A little boy. Dead. For a moment Jamie felt ashamed of herself. But only for a moment. She still clung to the thought that there could be nothing really good about Sylvia. Most likely she had killed her only child by being careless, driving under the influence or something foolish like that. "How did it happen?"

Her father sat back now and shook his head sadly. "The boy was in nursery school. Sylvia was in a car pool with two of her neighbors who had kids in the same school. One of them was driving that morning. Apparently some man ran a red light and smashed into them. They were all badly hurt, but only the little boy died."

How awful, Jamie thought. At the same time she felt cheated that it wasn't Sylvia who was at fault. "That's sad," she said.

"Yes, it is. I suppose one never really gets over the shock of something like that."

He stared off into space and Jamie had the feeling he was thinking of his own loss—her mother. Somehow that made her feel a little more kindly toward Sylvia. She knew how it felt to lose someone so dear. "Is that why she got a divorce?"

"Oh, no. She was already divorced when it happened."

"Then why *did* she get a divorce?"

She recognized the strictly-between-client-and-lawyer look that washed over his face. "That's Sylvia's business, Kitten. I don't think I should be talking about it."

She could tell she would get no more out of him on that subject, so she tried another. "How come she lives in the Bristol Arms? That's a really seedy-looking place."

"She lives there because although it may be seedy-looking, it's in a good neighborhood and it's cheap."

"She must be a cheapskate then."

"There you go again, judging before you have any of the facts. Sylvia helps support her mother, who is a widow, and therefore the Bristol Arms is the best she can afford."

"Oh," Jamie said.

"So, you see, Kitten, things are not always what they seem on the surface. Neither are people. Sylvia wants you to come to lunch one day soon. You'll get a chance to see her seedy apartment for yourself."

Ms. Schuyler's voice intruded on Jamie's thoughts, carrying her from the night before into the present moment in class. "Gavin," Ms. Schuyler was saying, "it's your turn to read. Now remember, in the story about the quest of the Holy Grail, Arthur has asked Lancelot how he has fared. Lancelot is obviously agitated. Start with the line that begins 'Seven days I drove . . .' "

Jamie was sure that Gavin would ham up Tennyson's blank verse. To her surprise, Gavin played it straight and read:

> Seven days I drove along the dreary deep,
> And with me drove the moon and all the stars;
> And the wind fell, and on the seventh night
> I heard the shingle grinding in the surge,
> And felt the boat shock earth, and looking up,

48

Behold, the enchanted towers of Carbonek,
A castle like a rock upon a rock, . . .

The piece was a long one, and the Gavin reading it was a different Gavin from any Jamie had ever seen. Suddenly he was Lancelot, or thought he was, and he was on that quest and taking the whole class with him. And the journey was exciting. Wondrous, Jamie thought.

He finished the last line in almost a whisper, " '. . . and this quest was not for me.' " Then he was silent for a moment, almost as if he needed time to return to his own century. In the next instant, he was Gavin again, and making one of his stupid clown faces, holding his nose, obviously passing judgment on his own performance.

"You're too hard on yourself, Gavin," Ms. Schuyler said. "You were wonderful. I suspected there was a terrific actor hiding inside you."

That was the first time Jamie had ever seen Gavin blush. He turned bright pink and sat down without another word.

Ms. Schuyler said, "We might try dramatizing some of the other stories in *Idylls of the King*. Could be fun. And don't forget, class, Open House is on the fifteenth of this month. I expect to meet all your parents that night."

Open House. Jamie hadn't thought much about it until now. Now it seemed like a very good idea, indeed.

49

❧ 6 ❧

You Never Really
Know Anybody

"You know, Agnes, sometimes I think you never really know anybody," Jamie said as she sat sprawled in a chair at the kitchen table, studying the pink jelly bean she had just taken from the glass jar.

Agnes, who was breaking eggs into a bowl, said, "Who did what now?"

Jamie ignored the question. "Did you know my mother smoked?"

Agnes stopped what she was doing. "Not when I knew her."

"No, she'd quit by then, my dad said. But I just never knew that about her."

"There are probably a lot of things you never knew about her."

"I doubt that. Remember, Agnes, she was *my* mother," Jamie said indignantly.

"That's exactly what I mean. People aren't just mothers or fathers. They're lots of different people. You knew your mother as a mother. Your father knew her as a different person—a wife. And her friends knew her as someone else—a friend."

"But she was still the same person."

"Yes and no. Her friends knew a side of her that you could never know. And so did your father. Like I say, we're all many people."

"Is that why you never really know anybody?"

"You know as much about a person as they want you to know. People always have a right to keep a piece of themselves to themselves, I always say."

"Are you many different people, Agnes?"

"Of course I am. I'm one person with you, another with your daddy, another with Hector, and so on."

Jamie supposed that she must be many different people as well, although she had never thought of herself that way before. And what about Ms. Schuyler? Was she many different people, too? If so, Jamie wished that one day she would have the privilege of knowing all of them. "Agnes, do you think there are people who can find one of these different persons inside somebody—I mean, a good personality that nobody even knew they had—and maybe bring it to life?"

"Never gave it much thought," Agnes said, mixing the concoction in the bowl with her hands. "I suppose there are people like that. I guess that's what's called bringing out the best in somebody."

"You know what, Agnes?"

"What?"

"I think Ms. Schuyler's one of those people. I mean, the kind that brings out something new and good in people."

"Ms. Schuyler, Ms. Schuyler—Jamie, I have never heard you talk so much about anybody."

"That's because she's such a—an indescribable human being. She even knows how to bring out something good in Gavin."

"What do you mean?"

Jamie told her about what a fine reading Gavin had given that day. "Ms. Schuyler said she suspected there was a terrific actor hidden inside Gavin. And maybe there is, but nobody else knew it. I mean, she really knows how to get the best out of everybody."

"Must be some teacher."

"Oh, she is, Agnes. She's, well, she's just indescribable."

Agnes said, "Are you going to sit and stare at that jelly bean all afternoon?"

Jamie put the candy in her mouth and sucked on it. "You know something else, Agnes?"

"No, what?"

"I've got it figured out why my dad and Sylvia are friends."

"Friends, are they?" Agnes sounded doubtful.

Annoyed, Jamie said, "It's just friendship, Agnes— really. And you know why?"

"No, why?"

"Because they're both bereaved. They've both lost a loved one."

"I thought she was divorced," Agnes said.

"Oh, it wasn't her husband. It was her little boy. He was killed in an auto accident."

Agnes gasped. "The poor thing . . . Oh, that's sad."

"Yes. And no one can understand something like that unless they've been through it themselves. So that's why they're friends. They're consoling each other."

"That's all, huh?"

"Of course."

"Don't bet on it."

"Oh, Agnes . . ." How could Agnes possibly understand? She had never lost a loved one. "It's like therapy, Agnes. Remember how I couldn't talk about it after my mother died, and Daddy sent me to that psychologist?"

Agnes nodded.

"Well, it was easier to talk about it to a stranger, and when I did, I felt better. Daddy never went to anybody though. And most likely Sylvia didn't either. So now they can talk about it to each other, and that's why they're friends."

"And when they get all the talk out of their systems, what then?"

Jamie thought about that. "Well, I suppose it's like me with the psychologist. When I felt better, I didn't need her anymore."

Agnes packed the makings for meatloaf into a baking dish. Jamie caught a whiff of spices and garlic. "What kind of muffins do you want tonight?" Agnes asked.

"How about bran?"

"Bran it is." Agnes put the meatloaf into the already heated oven and set the timer. She took a clean mixing bowl from a cupboard. Before she started on the muffins, she turned to Jamie, a worried expression on her face. "Jamie, I know you'd like to rearrange the world and everyone in it to suit your own ideas, but you can't. Things don't always fall into place the way you want them to."

Surprised, Jamie said, "I don't know what you mean, Agnes."

"I mean—" Agnes broke off. "Forget it. Maybe I'm wrong."

Of course Agnes was wrong, Jamie thought. She wasn't trying to rearrange anything or anybody. Agnes was smart enough usually, but sometimes she just didn't have quite as much insight and understanding as Jamie.

Agnes started taking ingredients from the cupboard and measuring for muffins. When she spooned out sugar from the canister on the counter, she said, "How'd the jelly bean get in here?"

"I don't know," Jamie said, not much interested.

Agnes shrugged. "Oh, well . . ." She fished the candy out and popped it into her mouth.

Jamie said, "I guess I'll go do some homework," and took off for her room. At her desk, she stared down at her algebra book, but her mind was back in Ms. Schuyler's class. She liked the way, when there was no one else around, Ms. Schuyler called her Cassandra-Jamie.

Once long ago she'd looked up the name Cassandra in the library, but she couldn't remember much of what she'd read. Now she decided to check the big dictionary in her father's study. She hurried to the room and turned the pages until she found:

Cassandra, n. Also called Alexandra.

Jamie's mouth dropped open. Oh, wow! This was really mind-blowing. She quickly read the rest:

CLASS. MYTH. a daughter of Priam and Hecuba, a prophetess cursed by Apollo so that her prophecies, although true, were fated never to be believed.

Coincidence? No way. Alexandra and Cassandra. One and the same. She and Ms. Schuyler were clearly destined to meet. She could hardly wait until tomorrow to tell her. Right now, she hurried to the kitchen to share her discovery with Agnes.

Agnes was just sliding a muffin tin into the oven. She closed the door, placed the cover on the sugar canister.

Jamie opened her mouth to say *You know something, Agnes?* but as she watched Agnes reposition the canister on the counter, a strange thought flashed through her head. She said, "Agnes, what color was that jelly bean you found in the sugar?"

Agnes thought for a second. "Believe it was orange. What difference does it make?"

Jamie puzzled over it for a moment, then said, "When Gavin borrowed sugar the other day, I dropped an orange jelly bean in his cup by mistake. When he returned the sugar yesterday, he must have brought back the very same cup of sugar."

"Of course," Agnes said. "Didn't you guess?"

Jamie was aghast. "You mean he always brings back the same sugar he borrows? Why would he do a thing like that? That's crazy."

"Not when you need an excuse to talk to someone."

"You mean he never makes candy? He just wants to visit? How weird."

"Well, he doesn't get much attention from that family of his. I think he's lonely. And don't you go letting on that you're wise. He's too proud to come barging over without an excuse."

Proud? Gavin? Lonely? Jamie couldn't believe it. Yet Agnes did. Jamie said, "You know, Agnes, sometimes I think you never really know anybody."

❧ 7 ❧

Open House

Alexandra and Cassandra. Alex and Cassandra. Alex and Cass. Alexandra and Cassie. Jamie tried all sorts of combinations that night after dinner. Alex and Cassandra sounded best to her.

Alex and Cassandra stroll, arm in arm, through the indescribable gardens at Versailles. Alex says, "Marie Antoinette walked these very paths."

"I know," Cassandra says. "Can't you just feel her presence?"

They both stand silent, sensing that the French queen is near, and the fragrance of the flowers is really her perfume. Oh, the beauty of this moment. This indescribable moment. This utterly indescribable moment.

Then Alex says, "There is so much I want you to see in France, little out-of-the-way places that tourists know nothing about. Then it's on to Rome where I want to show you wonders that will take your breath away."

Alex and Cassandra. They do something Cassandra has

always wanted to do. They stay up until the wee hours of the morning, talking and talking. Cassandra shares with Alex all her most beautiful and hidden thoughts, thoughts she has been saving up all her life.

Alex and Cassandra. Everyone stares at them and murmurs, "Oh, what beautiful people."

Jamie couldn't begin to fathom why Agnes didn't understand that there just had to be something magical about the fact that she and Ms. Schuyler both bore the name of the prophetess. "Lots of people have those names," Agnes said. Sometimes Agnes didn't have any imagination at all. And she wasn't a bit romantic.

Jamie hated waiting until the next day to tell the teacher about her astounding discovery. She went to the desk in her bedroom and pulled out the phone number of the house where Ms. Schuyler was staying. Her father was out again with Sylvia, so she went to his study to use the phone there. That way Agnes wouldn't hear her.

What would she say? *I was just looking up a word in the dictionary and I just happened to notice the name Cassandra there.* What if Ms. Schuyler asked her what word she was looking up?

She went to her father's big dictionary and thumbed through it until she found *Cassandra* again. After going over the words above and below the name, she finally settled on *casque*, which was some kind of medieval helmet.

I was reading this book about medieval times when I came across the word casque. I looked it up in the dictionary and found . . . Yes, that would do it.

She dialed the number written on the paper and waited to hear Ms. Schuyler's low, throaty voice. Instead, the voice that answered was high and shrill, definitely not Ms. Schuyler. Somehow that brought Jamie to her senses. Ms. Schuyler might not like someone bothering her at home.

"Hello, hello— Is anyone there?" the person demanded.

Jamie hung up. She would have to wait, savoring the knowledge all by herself for one night.

The next day Jamie had to contain herself through all her other classes and through English as well. Trudy Kirsh was home with a cold, so there were no explanations to make after the bell sounded.

Jamie hurried up to Ms. Schuyler's desk and breathlessly said, "Could I—" She stopped to correct herself. "May I see you for a minute, Ms. Schuyler?"

The teacher glanced at her quizzically. "Of course, Jamie. What's up?"

She had rehearsed the words so carefully. Now her mind almost went blank. She collected herself and said, "I just had to tell you. Yesterday afternoon I just happened to be looking up this word in the dictionary. Actually, the word was *casque*." Jamie suddenly realized that

59

Ms. Schuyler might think she meant *cask*, and of course she wouldn't be looking up a word anybody would know. "That's spelled c-a-s-q-u-e. It's a medieval helmet. Well, I just happened to be looking it up. Then I just happened to notice my name a little below it."

Ms. Schuyler looked puzzled. "Your name—Jamie?"

Ms. Schuyler surely couldn't have forgotten. "Oh, no. You see, I was in the Cs." She waited.

"Oh, of course—Cassandra."

"You know what it said?"

"That she was a prophetess, etcetera?"

"Yes, it said all that. But it said something else, too. It said"—Jamie paused for dramatic effect—"it said 'also called Alexandra.'"

A look of amusement passed over Ms. Schuyler's face. "How did you know my name?"

Jamie felt her face get hot. She didn't want Ms. Schuyler to think she had done something underhanded. "I just happened to see it typed on an envelope one of the teachers asked me to give you once."

"Oh, yes. I remember."

"Did you know that about Cassandra and Alexandra?"

"No, I didn't. That's interesting, isn't it?"

Jamie nodded. She waited for the teacher to say something significant, then decided that she was probably too overcome.

Finally, Ms. Schuyler gave Jamie a nice crinkly smile

and said, "Well, now, that practically makes us relatives, doesn't it?"

Oh frabjous day! as Lewis Carroll's nonsense poem went. She knew! Ms. Schuyler knew, just as Jamie knew. They were bonded. Destiny had declared them bonded.

All the rest of that day Jamie had a nice warm feeling, something like coming home and finding someone you belong to, and who belongs to you, waiting there to hug you.

Long before the fifteenth of the month Jamie had made her father promise that he would be available for Open House. She reminded him over and over for fear that he might forget and make another engagement. With Sylvia, probably. Then he'd most likely insist on dragging her along, and that would be a disaster!

When the night finally came, her father was late getting home. Waiting for him, Jamie grew more hurt and angry by the second. "If he breaks his promise to me, Agnes," she said, "I'll never speak to him again."

"Calm down," Agnes said. "When has he ever broken a promise to you? There's plenty of time. Besides, if he wasn't coming home he'd have called."

"No, there isn't plenty of time. He'll have to eat and change. We'll never get there."

"Why does he have to change? Your daddy always looks nice."

"Agnes, you can't wear a three-piece suit to an Open House at school! That's tacky. You have to look casual." Jamie, herself, was wearing new jeans and a rough-textured silk sweater. You had to look casual, but not too casual. She had already picked out her father's outfit, one that she felt would make him look less fatherly. He was also to wear jeans, but with a bulky, cotton knit sweater. They would look wonderful together. Pals out for a carefree evening, having fun. Making the right impression on Ms. Schuyler was so important.

Her father arrived in plenty of time to eat, and, good-naturedly, he changed into the clothes she had chosen for him to wear. Then he said, "I don't remember ever wearing jeans to an Open House at school before. Are you sure I won't be making a bad impression?"

"Oh, no, Daddy. You look wonderful. It's tacky to be overdressed—it really is." The only time Jamie wore what she thought of as formal clothes was on those Fridays she had Cotillion. Then, everyone dressed up.

When they arrived at school, her father made a point of calling her attention to every other father in a business suit and tie. "Tacky," Jamie said of each of them.

"If you say so," he said.

Jamie ushered him around, introducing him to her teachers, showing him the displays of students' work. She was so proud of him. He knew exactly the right things to say to everyone. At one point she tried to look at him through her girlfriend's eyes. Did he look sexy? She just couldn't tell.

Naturally she saved Ms. Schuyler's room until last. By that time, there were fewer people around. When they walked in, Gavin and his parents were talking to her, so Jamie led her father around the room, showing him the papers Ms. Schuyler had displayed on bulletin boards.

"Oh, look," he said, "here's one by Jamie Cole. What do you know!"

Of course Jamie had known that her definition of poetry was a part of the display, but she felt shy about pointing it out. As he read it, she stood by anxiously.

"Why, that's lovely." He put an arm around her and gave her an affectionate squeeze. "I always knew you were smart, Kitten, but I didn't know you were a poet."

"That's not poetry, Daddy."

"Oh, yes, it is. And very good poetry, too."

Jamie was so happy. Ever since he'd been seeing Sylvia Dennis, he had spent less and less time with Jamie. She missed him, missed the special camaraderie they had when they were alone together. A long time had passed since he'd said, "Let's have a father-daughter night. We'll go someplace for dinner, then take in a show. How about it?" Now, instead of taking *her*, he took Sylvia.

She didn't have time to dwell on that thought, because they had now made their way around the room and were

63

closer to Ms. Schuyler and the MacLarens. She could hear Gavin's mother saying, "I know how exasperating he is. Sometimes I'm at my wit's end."

"Oh, I didn't mean that," Ms. Schuyler said. "I think Gavin has high spirits, yes, but he also has talent. I think he'd make a very good actor."

His father said, "Actor, huh?"

"Sometimes I wish he'd been born a girl," his mother said. "Caroline is no trouble at all. I just don't know how to manage boys."

"Girl?" Gavin said, and acted as though he were giving it serious thought. "I'll work on it."

Ms. Schuyler laughed, which seemed to relieve a tension that promised to build. She glanced toward Jamie and her father. All of the MacLarens' eyes followed hers and lit upon them with recognition. There were a few moments of *Hi, neighbor, how y'doing?* with a lot of *fine, fine, fine*s all around. Then the MacLarens turned their spot over to the Coles and made their way toward the door.

Jamie said, "Ms. Schuyler, I'd like you to meet my dad." She kept watching him and was disappointed to see no flicker of recognition in his eyes.

"I'm so happy to meet you, Mr. Cole," Ms. Schuyler said and extended a hand to shake his. "I can't tell you what a pleasure it is for a teacher to have a fine student like Jamie in her class."

64

"Jamie's always done well in English," Richard Cole said. "She was reading on her own before she ever started school."

To Jamie's embarrassment, her dad spent what seemed like ages bragging about her accomplishments. She kept saying, "Oh, Dad," but nothing would stop him. At the same time, she was pleased to have Ms. Schuyler hear all the good things about her and see how much her dad thought of her. Finally, she decided she couldn't just stand there and let him praise her all night, so she said, "Daddy, you're exaggerating."

He glanced at her and looked surprised. "Am I?" Then he grinned. "No, I'm not. Haven't I always told you you take after me?"

They all laughed. Then it was Jamie's turn. "You should hear my dad play piano, Ms. Schuyler. Everybody says he has a natural talent. He can play anything."

"Not quite," he put in.

"Jazz?" Ms. Schuyler asked.

"My favorite," he said.

She said, "I love jazz piano."

They talked for a while about their favorite old-time jazz musicians. At length, he said, "Well, Jamie, I think it's time our mutual admiration society went off and gave someone else a chance."

Jamie wanted to prolong the meeting, but there *were* other families waiting.

"Nice to meet you, Mr. Cole," Ms. Schuyler said with one of her big smiles.

"My pleasure," he responded and took Jamie's arm and led her away as Ms. Schuyler turned to greet someone else.

In the car on the way home, Jamie asked, "Daddy, who does Ms. Schuyler remind you of?"

"I don't know. Why? Should she remind me of someone?"

How exasperating he was. "Yes."

"Well, let me think. Someone in the movies?"

"No, no, no! Someone much closer."

"Closer, eh?" He shook his head. "I'm drawing a blank, Kitten. You'd better tell me."

Jamie couldn't believe it. "Mother!"

He took his eyes from the road just long enough to give her a quick, astonished look. "Your mother? Well, I guess you could say her hair is about the same color. And she's probably about the same size. Other than that, I can't see any resemblance."

Jamie was appalled. How could her father, in three years' time, have forgotten so completely what her mother looked like? She could only think of one reason—Sylvia Dennis.

❧ 8 ❧

The Beautiful People
Are All Vegetarians

In English the next day, Ms. Schuyler decided that for
their big class project the students would write and act in
a dramatization of the story of "Lancelot and Elaine,"
from *Idylls of the King*.

"We'll divide it into scenes," she said. "I want you to
pair up, two of you working together on each scene. We'll
use a narrator to read the parts that we don't act out.
When you've all finished writing your scenes, we'll put the
whole thing together and see what needs smoothing out."

Jamie heard only dimly. Her mind was on what she and
her father had talked about the night before. She was still
annoyed that he didn't seem to remember what her
mother had looked like. If he could only see Ms. Schuyler
again, the memory would return just as it had with Jamie.
After all, that brief meeting in school wasn't really enough
to take in anybody. You had to be around a person a while
to catch all their little mannerisms.

"Don't you think Ms. Schuyler's nice?" she'd asked her
father when they returned home.

"Very nice," he said.

"She's a wonderful teacher."

"I'm sure she is."

"I mean, Daddy, she's the kind of teacher that a person might have only once in their whole life."

"That good, eh?"

"Indescribably good."

"That's *really* got to be good. At any rate, it's obvious you like her."

"Oh, I do." Jamie suddenly had a great idea. "Daddy, why don't we ask her to dinner?"

"Dinner?" he said, sounding surprised. "You mean take her out to some restaurant?"

"No. At home."

"I don't know, Kitten. That would be more work for Agnes."

"Agnes wouldn't mind. She loves to make dinner for company." In truth, Jamie had no idea how Agnes felt about company coming to dinner, but because she had never complained about the task, Jamie reasoned, she must like it.

He still hesitated. "Well, I just don't know. I mean, when I was a kid in school, it never occurred to me to ask a teacher to my home for dinner, even the ones I really liked."

"But those were the olden days, Daddy."

"I know. I'm medieval."

"I didn't mean that. You know what I meant."

"Only too well. But that's neither here nor there. What makes you think she'd want to come?"

"Oh, I know she would, Daddy. Did you hear what she said when you said jazz was your favorite? She said, 'I love jazz piano.' I think she was hinting that she wanted to hear you play. I think she likes you."

Her father grinned. "Jamie, how you overestimate my fatal charm. And how I love it. Oh, well, if it means so much to you, go ahead and ask your teacher to dinner, but be sure and check with Agnes first."

"And you've got to promise to come home on time that night and not bring anybody else."

"Of course I'll be here."

"Promise."

He had sighed deeply and raised his right hand. "I promise. Cross my heart and hope to die."

Now, Jamie thought with satisfaction, everything was going beautifully. She had checked with Agnes that very morning. Agnes said, "Why not? Doesn't hurt to butter up the teacher." Then they discussed the wonderful delicacies they might serve.

The sound of Ms. Schuyler's voice calling her name brought Jamie back to the present. "Gavin says you live close to him," she was saying. "That will make working together easier."

Jamie frowned. She could hardly admit that she hadn't been listening and ask Ms. Schuyler for a rundown on what was going on. Sadly enough, she could guess anyhow. Somehow she'd been paired with Gavin.

Ms. Schuyler said, "You two can take the opening scene with Arthur, Guinevere, and Lancelot, up to the point where Guinevere convinces Lancelot that he must be part of the yearly diamond jousts."

Jamie was so angry with herself for daydreaming. Had she been attentive, she would never have found herself in this fix. She listened carefully now as Ms. Schuyler assigned pages to the other students. Apparently they were to rewrite them in play form, using as many of Tennyson's lines as was possible or sensible. They were all paired and were to work together on their own time, at their own convenience.

"As the old saw goes, 'Two heads are better than one.' " Ms. Schuyler went on talking about the work, making it sound very exciting. Jamie might have felt some enthusiasm if she wasn't stuck with Gavin for a partner.

Trudy Kirsch was over her cold and back in school now, so when the bell finally rang, Jamie said to her, "You'd better go on to gym, Trudy. I just have to ask Ms. Schuyler something about the assignment."

Trudy said, "It seems to me you always have to ask Ms.

Schuyler something about something. What gives, anyhow?"

"Nothing. It's just that I'm not clear about something, that's all. Go ahead. I'll be along in a minute."

"Oh, all right," Trudy said, sounding annoyed.

When she left, Jamie made for Ms. Schuyler's desk. This was the moment she had been waiting for all day.

The teacher was sitting down now, going through some papers. She glanced up at Jamie and said, "Cassandra-Jamie, you have a very determined look on your face. What's up?"

Jamie plunged ahead and said breathlessly, "I was wondering if you could come to dinner at my house next Wednesday night."

For a moment Ms. Schuyler's eyes rested on Jamie with an expression Jamie couldn't read. At length she said, "I'm sorry, Jamie, but I'm afraid I can't."

Jamie thought she had probably chosen the wrong night. "Oh, it doesn't have to be Wednesday if that's not convenient. We can make it another night. Agnes won't mind. She's our housekeeper. She'll make something really special like paella." She thought a dish with a gourmet-sounding name would really impress Ms. Schuyler. When the expected response didn't show in her eyes, Jamie quickly added, "Or we could have lobster or steak—or both—or whatever your favorite is."

Ms. Schuyler smiled now. "Jamie, I'm a vegetarian."

Taken aback, Jamie said, "Oh."

"I don't accept many dinner invitations because it gives people too much trouble."

"Not Agnes," Jamie said, recovered now. "She wouldn't mind. She makes a wonderful vegetable dish with zucchini and mushrooms and tomatoes and cheese. And her eight-layer chocolate cake is out of this world."

"No, Jamie, I'm afraid not."

"My dad will play jazz piano for you if you want. He said he thought you were very nice."

"And he's very nice. And you're very nice. But the answer is still no. The truth is, Jamie, as a teacher, I don't want to do anything that would either consciously or unconsciously affect the way I grade my students. Do you understand?"

"I guess so," Jamie said, although she really didn't. She *did* understand, though, that Ms. Schuyler wasn't about to compromise her principles.

"I'm really sorry, Jamie, but thank you for asking me anyhow. I'm very flattered."

The room was starting to fill with students so Jamie had to leave. She felt disappointed, yet not defeated. On the way to the gym she promised herself she'd just have to find some new strategy that would work better.

Later that day, when Jamie came home from school, she told Agnes about the teacher's reason for refusing. Agnes

72

said, "I sure don't understand how anyone could accuse her of giving you a better grade than you'd earned when you earn top grades anyhow."

"Just the same, Agnes, you have to admire someone who has principles and sticks to them."

"Well, come to think of it, she's probably right. After one of my gourmet meals, she'd be bound to feel beholden to the Cole household for life. And you wouldn't want the kids at school calling you teacher's pet, now would you?"

Jamie gave a half-smile, but the truth was she wouldn't have minded at all. *Alex and Cassandra, the beautiful people, were above feeling resentment just because the rest of the world was jealous of their relationship.*

That same afternoon Gavin came over without the usual measuring cup in his hand.

"No sugar today?" Agnes asked.

"Not today, Lady Agnes." He sounded all business as he turned to Jamie and said, "When can we get together on this play thing?"

"There's lots of time," Jamie said.

"Yeah, but I'd like to get it out of my hair."

Jamie said, "I don't want to do it after school. I have too much homework. It'll have to be on a weekend."

"Okay. Make it Saturday afternoon." He glanced down at his wristwatch. "What time do you have?"

Jamie looked at hers. "Four-thirty-five."

"Good. We're synchronized. I'll be here at two o'clock

sharp." He strode over to Agnes, who was stirring a sauce fragrant with the smell of vanilla. He took the spoon from her hand, put her hand to his lips, and kissed it. "Farewell, Lady Agnes." To Jamie, he doffed an imaginary hat and made a deep bow. "Farewell, fair princess. We shall meet again three days hence at the stroke of two."

Jamie said, "Gavin, you are really too much."

He raised his hands in mock protest. "No, no. Don't make a fuss over me. Just treat me as you would any other great man." He turned on his heel and marched out the door.

When he'd gone, Agnes asked, "What's all this two-o'clock business?"

Jamie told her about the project that had paired her with Gavin. Agnes said, "That sounds like something that ought to be right up his alley."

"Maybe so, but I don't know how I'm going to stand working with him. He's such a pain."

"He's a cut-up all right, but I guess you'll just have to put up with him."

Jamie sighed, feeling sorry for herself. Then Gavin disappeared from her mind and Ms. Schuyler filled it. "Agnes, what are we having for dinner?"

"Salad, roast beef, stuffed potato-skins, broccoli, and pudding with my special sauce."

"What's in the potato skins?"

"My secret filling."

"Any meat?"

"No, why?"

"I guess I'll just have the salad and vegetables and dessert. From now on, Agnes, I'm going to start eating vegetarian."

In the same tone she'd recited the list of dishes for dinner, Agnes said, "Over my dead body."

"But, Agnes, lots of people are vegetarians."

"When you grow up and do your own cooking and learn how to put together a balanced diet without meat, you can be a vegetarian. I am not about to learn a new way of cooking so that you can get the proper proteins. You can't eat just any bunch of vegetables, you know, and stay healthy."

No, Jamie didn't know. Well, tonight she'd eat what Agnes gave her. In the future though she'd make it her business to learn all about vegetarianism. Then she'd have the ammunition to fight Agnes.

Alex and Cassandra, the beautiful people. They're vegetarians, you know.

✤ 9 ✤

A New Plan

Gavin had arrived at two o'clock sharp on Saturday, just as he'd promised, and he and Jamie had settled into the family room. Her father was out playing golf, and Agnes and Hector were having a late lunch in the kitchen.

Gavin wasted no time in getting down to business. "This is how we'll do it," he said, taking charge. "We use a narrator for the opening, starting with 'Elaine the fair, Elaine the lovable,/Elaine, the lily maid of Astolat,' and on through the part about how Arthur found the diamonds that the knights jousted for every year."

Jamie, annoyed that he seemed to have worked out everything without her, said, "Why do we have to start with a narrator?"

"Well, for one thing, Tennyson didn't use any dialogue here, and for another—"

Jamie broke in. "We could write the dialogue. We can take some of the lines and have Elaine say them." Carried away with her own cleverness, she continued, "Elaine is guarding Lancelot's shield while he's gone to joust. She's dreaming about him while she takes in every mark on it.

76

She could say something like . . ." Jamie glanced at the words in the book, "like, 'Fair Lord, what sword made this dint, what lance this scratch?' "

"Fair lord!" Gavin exclaimed. "Yuk."

Indignant, Jamie said, "That just happens to be what she calls him," and thumbed through until she found the spot. "Look." She pointed to the words.

Gavin glanced at the page and shrugged "That's what it says all right. I guess I just read over it."

"And look here." Jamie pointed to another section. "Here she calls him *noble lord*. That's how they talk."

"Okay, okay. He can be *fair lord*. But not here. You didn't let me finish what I was saying. Ms. Schuyler said this part should be narrated. Didn't you hear her?"

Remembering how she'd been dreaming that day, Jamie said, "I guess I missed that. Well, if that's the way she wants it, I guess she must have a reason."

"Okay. Then we start with Arthur, Guinevere, and Lancelot talking about the diamond joust. Arthur asks the queen if she's too sick to go. She says yes."

Jamie interrupted. "She says, 'Yea, lord.' "

"Yeah. And Lancelot thinks she wants him to stay with her because she loves him, so he tells the king that his old wound is kicking up. The trouble is some of the lines of dialogue go on and on like long speeches. We'll just have to break them up."

They worked all afternoon, totally engrossed, arguing

over lines of dialogue and where and how they should break them, and whether Lancelot should throw in a few *uh huhs* to break the queen's long speeches, and whether *uh huhs* were even used in the world of Camelot.

Finally, at about four-thirty, Agnes brought in a tray with glasses of milk and a plate of freshly baked brownies. "From the sound of the two of you, I thought you might be running out of fuel. How's it going, anyhow?"

"Pretty good," Gavin said. "It would go better if Jamie didn't think every word was engraved in gold. I have to fight for each crumby change."

"Well, I just like things to be right the first time," Jamie said.

"You know, you're the kind of person who'd do crossword puzzles with a pen. You've got to realize things like this are never right the first time. You've just got to keep working them over until they are."

"You're a perfectionist," Agnes said to him.

"I don't know what he is," Jamie said, "but he wears me out." She was surprised to find that Gavin took this project much more seriously than she did.

"Okay," he said. "We won't do any more today. I'll type up a rough copy of what we have. Then we can read the lines out loud and see if they work."

"And if they don't?"

"We'll change them."

"That's what I was afraid of," Jamie said.

Agnes pushed aside books and papers to set the tray on the low table in front of the sofa where they sat side by side. "Help yourself and bring out the dishes when you're finished. As for me, I've got things to do," she said and headed back to the kitchen.

They each took one of Agnes's brownies. Biting into his, Gavin said, "Agnes sure bakes a mean brownie."

"She's a good cook," Jamie said.

As they ate, Gavin asked, "Are you going to Cotillion this month?" Cotillion was one of the few places where Gavin shone. He was the best dancer of all the boys.

"Of course," Jamie said, "I always go."

"They asked my dad and mom to chaperone next month, but they couldn't make it."

Jamie thought he looked relieved.

"My mom says Ms. Schuyler is filling in for her."

Jamie's ears perked up. "Who's filling in for your dad?"

Gavin shrugged. "So far, nobody. I guess they're still looking for somebody, though."

O frabjous day! Destiny was taking the situation in hand again. Now Jamie knew why fate had paired her with Gavin.

To Jamie's surprise, Gavin said, "You know, that Schuyler is okay."

"Okay!" Jamie exclaimed. "She's indescribably better

79

than that. She's a beautiful person and a wonderful teacher."

"Yeah, she's okay." When Jamie gave him a disgusted look, he said, "Indescribably okay?"

Jamie knew very well that, for Gavin, that was high praise. And if he had the ability to appreciate Ms. Schuyler then he couldn't be *all* bad. She thought of the cup of sugar that traveled back and forth between their houses. How sad, how unutterably sad that seemed now. For the first time she felt a little sorry for Gavin.

When Gavin left, Jamie took the tray of dirty dishes to the kitchen, where Agnes was preparing dinner. She put the tray where it belonged and the dishes in the dishwasher. "The brownies were delicious, Agnes."

"Good."

As Agnes checked the bean pot in the oven, Jamie asked, "What time did my dad say he'd be home?"

Agnes closed the oven door and glanced up at the kitchen clock on the wall. "He should be in any minute now."

Jamie could hardly wait.

Agnes said, "How did you make out, working with Gavin?"

"Better than I thought. He doesn't fool around when he's working. It's too bad he can't be that way all the time."

"Oh, he'll outgrow those antics of his when he gets older."

"Maybe," Jamie said doubtfully. "But in the meantime..."

"In the meantime, we'll just have to bear with him. What are you two writing about, anyhow?"

"We're making a play out of the story of Lancelot, who was in King Arthur's court, and Elaine, the lily maid of Astolat."

"What's it about?"

"Oh, it's sad, Agnes. You see, Elaine is in love with Lancelot, but he's in love with Guinevere, the queen. Elaine dies for love of him, but before she does, she makes her father promise to put her dead body on a barge with a servant to row her to Arthur's court.

"And the barge is draped in black, Agnes, and Elaine is all in white with a lily in one hand and a letter bidding Lancelot farewell in the other. When all the people in the court see her, they cry because she's so beautiful and so young. And Lancelot feels awful."

"That Elaine was a pretty smart cookie," Agnes said. "She might not have gotten her man, but she knew how to make him feel guilty for the rest of his life."

"You're not supposed to look at it like that, Agnes. It's like a Greek tragedy."

"Oh, I see—high drama."

Before Jamie could educate Agnes further, she heard

the sound of the front door closing and knew her father had come home at last. She forgot all about the story and ran to the entry hall to meet him.

When he saw her, he said, "Hi, Kitten," and placed a kiss on the middle of her forehead.

"There's something I've got to ask you, Daddy."

"First, let me put away these clubs." He made his way to a hall closet that held a hodgepodge of sports equipment, clothing, and odds and ends. Jamie waited patiently as he squeezed in the bag of golf clubs. "Someday I'm just going to have to clean out this closet," he said.

Jamie couldn't imagine why he had not been at all disturbed when Ms. Schuyler had refused to come for dinner. "Probably wise of her," was all he said. But then, he'd really had no chance to get to know her. Cotillion would take care of that. She said, "Daddy, you've just got to volunteer for Cotillion next month."

"Volunteer? As what?"

"Chaperone, of course. All the parents do it. They take turns."

"And it's my turn?"

"Well—well, yes."

"Who decides all this?"

"Well, *they* do."

"Ah, that nice anonymous *they*."

"Please, Daddy, you've got to."

He gave a tolerant sigh. "All right, Kitten. If I must, I

must. We'll talk about it at dinner. You can tell me what I have to do. Right now, I want to shower and change."

Jamie was so pleased. Everything was working out beautifully.

Her father started toward his bedroom, then turned back to her. "Oh, by the way, Sylvia's on vacation next week. She's driving up to Oregon to see her mother for a few days, but she'll be back by Saturday. She wants you to have lunch with her at her apartment."

Rats, Jamie thought. She felt a little like Alice, running with the Red Queen. *Said the queen, "Now here, you see, it takes all the running you can do, to keep in the same place."*

❧ 10 ❧

When My Mother Was Alive

After the neglected appearance of Sylvia's building, her apartment came as a real surprise to Jamie. It was spacious and made you feel as if you were outdoors. The wallpaper, patterned with green leaves and delicate tree branches, had a white fence pictured at the bottom with real trellis work here and there that extended to the ceiling. There was lots of white wicker furniture strewn with cushions, some covered with a deep blue calico print, others white with red stripes down the center. Red and white carnations in glass vases lent another splash of color. Jamie had the feeling she was on the porch of some lovely old summer home.

Her own home had sensible, comfortable furniture without a touch of whimsy. And all of her friends had homes with the kind of furniture you never noticed. It was simply there, and everything was just what it seemed to be. A chair was a chair, and a table was a table. Sylvia had taken things and made them into something else. For instance, what had obviously been a huge china urn decorated with blue, Oriental designs, now held a round glass top that turned it into a small table. The whole room looked fresh and clean and summery.

"When I first walked in, for a minute, I almost thought I was outdoors," Jamie said to Sylvia over lunch.

"It doesn't really fool the eye," Sylvia said, "but I find it does have a way of fooling the senses."

Jamie had to agree. "One summer when my mother was still alive, we visited my aunt and uncle in Connecticut. They have an old-fashioned house in the country with a big porch—actually, they call it a veranda—with trees all around. Your apartment reminds me of it." Then she realized that Sylvia might be offended to hear that her living room looked like a porch, so Jamie added, "It's nice."

"I hoped you'd like it," Sylvia said, then changed the subject. "You must miss your mother very much, Jamie."

The words surprised Jamie. She had assumed that Sylvia would talk about anything and anyone except her mother. "Yes, I do," she said. Now that Sylvia had broached the subject, Jamie felt free to enlarge upon it. "She was English. Did you know that?"

"No, I didn't."

"She came over here when she was eleven, and she went to school here, but she never *did* lose her accent. Daddy used to tease her about it."

"I guess accents aren't easy to lose."

Jamie nodded. She took another mouthful of the unfamiliar chicken dish on her plate and said, "This is really good."

Sylvia smiled. "I have a very good chef."

Jamie glanced toward the kitchen, half expecting someone like Agnes to appear.

"Stouffer's," Sylvia said.

If Sylvia used frozen dishes, Jamie decided, she mustn't like to cook. Jamie said, "When my mother was alive, we always had gourmet meals. She loved to cook." Agnes kept telling her that wasn't quite the case, but Jamie refused to believe her. Agnes said her mother was a sporadic cook who, once a week or so, would take over the kitchen and cook an elaborate meal that took hours of preparation. The rest of the time the kitchen belonged to Agnes. Strangely enough, Jamie remembered none of Agnes's meals from that time, only her mother's. "She used to like to experiment. We had wonderful meals all the time."

"I'm sure you miss her very much," Sylvia said again.

"Yes. Everything was so different when she was alive. Every summer we took great vacations. The year before she died we went up to Victoria in Canada. Mother said it made her feel she was back in England." Jamie sighed. "We haven't done anything like that since. Last summer I went to camp, but I didn't like it."

"I know the feeling. I never did like camp when I was

a kid. Even with all those people around me, I found it the loneliest place in the world."

Jamie glanced up, surprised. That was exactly the way she'd felt. You were never alone, but you were always lonely. The fact that Sylvia shared her feelings annoyed her rather than pleased her. She could have justified her resentment of the woman if Sylvia had said something like, *You should have tried harder to make friends* or *Next time you'll love it.* Jamie said, "I'm not going this year."

"Smart girl. There are lots of wonderful things to do in the summer besides going to camp. For me, it was always a time to catch up on my reading." Sylvia got up to clear away their dishes. "I have raspberry sherbet and cookies. Will that be enough for you?"

Jamie nodded. "Sounds good."

Sylvia disappeared into the kitchen. After a few minutes, she returned with their dessert. "I don't dare keep anything rich and gooey in the house because I know I couldn't resist the temptation. I'd soon be size sixteen."

Jamie thought Sylvia was model-thin already. She was wearing one of those long T-shirt dresses that made her look casual and elegant at the same time. Jamie conceded that it was probably an okay look, but all in all, she preferred Ms. Schuyler's outdoorsy look. Reminded of her teacher, she said, "You know, it's the strangest thing, I have this teacher who's the image of my mother. You just wouldn't believe it. It's really uncanny."

"Oh?"

Jamie could tell she had Sylvia's full attention now. "She's a wonderful teacher and the kind of person who brings out the best in everybody. I just love her."

"She sounds like quite a woman."

"Oh, she is. My dad thinks she's really nice."

"Oh?"

"Oh, yes. They're both going to be chaperones at Cotillion this month." Jamie thought she detected the slightest frown on Sylvia's face.

Sylvia said, "Cotillion—is that ballroom dancing?"

"Yes. We have an instructor and we learn all the dances. Last month it was the cha-cha. Agnes, our house-keeper, says it's a good way to get to know people of the opposite sex."

"I imagine it is."

Jamie thought Sylvia looked a little worried. "You know, I wouldn't be at all surprised if my dad was attracted to Ms. Schuyler, the teacher I've been telling you about. Agnes says that people who get divorced always turn right around and marry someone just like the person they divorced. I guess that's got to be even truer of widowers. And you wouldn't believe how much Ms. Schuyler looks and acts like my mother."

Now Sylvia really looked concerned. "Jamie, don't you think that's a bit of wishful thinking on your part?"

"Not really. I know they like each other, and that seems the most natural way for things to turn out."

Sylvia started to say something, then apparently thought better of it. Instead she got up. "I think I'll get some coffee. Would you like some more milk or anything?"

Jamie said no. In a few moments Sylvia returned with a steaming cup and took her place at the table again. For the first time since she'd entered the apartment Jamie realized that Sylvia hadn't smoked one cigarette. Was she refraining simply because she knew Jamie objected to smokers? Curious, Jamie said, "You can smoke if you want to. I don't mind."

Sylvia said, "I've stopped. For about the twentieth time. This time I think it's going to take."

Thinking of her mother, Jamie asked, "Did you go to a smokers' clinic?"

"No. One of my friends knew a hypnotist, and I've had several sessions with him. So far, it's working."

Jamie felt thoroughly irritated. Now she wouldn't even be able to object to being around Sylvia and breathing her secondhand smoke.

❦ 11 ❦

Gavin the Blackmailer

Jamie and Gavin had finished working on their scene for Ms. Schuyler's class and were celebrating in the kitchen with milk and some of Agnes's cookies. Gavin drained his glass and moved as though to toss it over his shoulder.

Agnes, who was enjoying a cup of tea with them, exclaimed, "Don't you dare, Gavin MacLaren!"

Gavin said, "But we're drinking a toast to a job well done, Lady Agnes. You always have to break the glass after a toast."

"That's only in the movies," Jamie said.

"Well, I don't care," he said, "our work deserves a couple of broken glasses. We did a brilliant job. Even Tennyson himself couldn't have done better."

Jamie's mind wasn't on their brilliant job but on the conversation she'd had with her father that morning.

"Jamie, you didn't tell me that the teacher you like so much is chaperoning at Cotillion this month," he'd said.

"Oh, didn't I?" Jamie said innocently.

"No, you didn't. And what I really want to know is why

you tried to give Sylvia the impression there was something between the woman and me."

"I didn't say any such thing! If she said that, she's
lying." What a snitch that Sylvia was turning out to be!
"All I said was you thought Ms. Schuyler was nice. After
all, you did say it. Those were your very words right after
you met her."

"They were?"

"Yes, they were," Jamie said firmly. "And all I wanted
was for you to get to know someone I really like. That's
not such a big deal, is it?"

"Maybe not, but why do I keep getting the feeling that
there's more here than meets the eye?"

"If you ask me, the *more* is that Sylvia is trying to make
trouble between us."

"No, that is not the case. Sylvia is not that kind of person. And, what's more, I won't have you saying things like
that."

"Then why did she tell you what she did?"

"Because she was genuinely concerned—about you."

I'll bet, Jamie thought. She was concerned all right, but
not about me. She was concerned that she might not get
you after all. And that was what she wanted, Jamie was
sure now. Or else why would she have asked her to lunch?
If you wanted to win the father, you had to win the
daughter. That was the way Agnes would have put it.

Marriage. That's what Sylvia wanted. Although Jamie

must have been unconsciously aware of this when she'd met Sylvia, she had never before put the thought into words. That first night at the restaurant she had merely resented Sylvia for sitting in the spot that had once belonged to her mother. Now that she had admitted to herself the possible, even probable, outcome of Sylvia's relationship with her father, Jamie was angry and deeply disturbed.

As she sat at the table with Gavin and Agnes, that was all that kept running through her head until she sputtered, "She wants to marry Daddy!"

They both stared at her with expressions of astonishment. "Who wants to marry your daddy?" Agnes asked.

"Sylvia."

"Who's Sylvia?" Gavin said.

"She's the woman my dad goes out with. She wants to marry him, I just know she does."

"That reminds me of a joke," Gavin said. "This guy with a new wife meets a friend and says, 'My wife's an angel.' The friend says, 'You're lucky, mine's still alive.' " When Jamie gave him a dirty look, he added, "Or how about this one—there was this woman who liked marriage so much her towels said His, Hers, and Next."

Jamie glared at him. "This is serious, Gavin. I'd appreciate it if you'd keep your jokes to yourself. I'm not in the mood."

Gavin threw up his hands in a just-trying-to-help gesture and shut up.

Agnes said to Jamie, "Is that what she told you when you had lunch with her?"

"Of course not. She's too sneaky for that. But you can bet that's what she wants, or else why would she bother to ask me to lunch?"

"Right," Agnes said. "How could she marry your father without getting your approval first?"

"You think you're joking, Agnes, but that's probably closer to the truth than you realize. And something else that I didn't tell you—she gave up smoking!"

Agnes shook her head solemnly. "No sacrifice too great, I guess."

"Agnes, I'm serious. You won't think it's funny when she takes over this house and starts cooking the way she does. All we'll have are frozen dinners and sherbet. And she'll throw out all the furniture, I know she will. There'll be nothing but white wicker all over the house."

"That does sound serious," Agnes said.

Gavin said, "I get the impression that you don't want your dad to marry again."

"It's not that I don't want him to marry again. I don't want him to marry just anybody."

"And I have a feeling that Sylvia isn't 'just anybody,'" Agnes said.

"I didn't really mean that the way it sounded. I just meant that she isn't the *right* person." And that was exactly the case. Sylvia simply wasn't the right person. And if she wasn't the right person, then it couldn't come to pass. With that thought, Jamie relaxed. "I guess it's silly to worry about it, though, because Sylvia just isn't a part of our destinies."

"Our destinies? Sounds like we'd all be marrying her," Agnes said.

"And that's so true, Agnes. Whoever Daddy marries, we all marry."

"That sounds illegal," Gavin said.

"You know what I mean, Gavin. She'd be as much a part of our lives as his. That's why it's so important to have the right person."

Gavin scratched his head. "I don't know. Maybe you ought to introduce Sylvia to my dad. Any change in my house would have to be for the better. As for frozen dinners, I get those anyhow. And Sylvia could take up smoking again because my dad smokes. She'd feel right at home."

"Gavin MacLaren," Agnes said, "you don't mean that."

Gavin grinned. "I guess I really don't. She's got her faults, but I'm so used to the drill sergeant yelling at me and telling me what to do that, without her, I'd probably have to wear a compass to know if I was coming or going."

Agnes said, "Jamie, you don't know this woman well

enough to go accusing her of being sneaky or under-handed."

"I know her well enough to know I don't like her."

Agnes said, "I don't think you do. You've seen her twice—once at lunch, once at dinner. That's not enough time to get to know anybody. She's probably a very nice person, or your daddy wouldn't be interested in her."

Jamie paid no heed to Agnes's words. "You know how she quit smoking? She's going to this hypnotist. If she knows someone like that, I'll bet she'll get the man to hypnotize Daddy and make him marry her."

Agnes shook her head despairingly. "Jamie, imagination is a nice gift, but a little can go a long way. And you've got too much for your own good."

"Besides," Gavin said, obviously trying to reassure Jamie, "I've heard that nobody can hypnotize anybody into doing anything they don't want to do."

"I sure hope not," Jamie said. "But I wouldn't put it past her to try."

Agnes leaned forward, wearing her stern look. "Now, Jamie, you listen to me. Your father is still a young man. He's been used to female companionship. It's only natural that he'd miss that and try to find it again. If this woman makes him happy, then we should all be happy for him. And if he wants to marry her, you're just going to have to learn to live with the situation."

Never, Jamie thought, but she said nothing. Agnes

95

would only go on lecturing her, and Jamie knew that no matter what anyone said, there was no way she would ever accept that woman as her father's wife.

In Ms. Schuyler's class the next day, the students read the work they had dramatized. Jamie and Gavin had taken the opening scene, so they were first. Gavin took the roles of King Arthur and Lancelot, and was narrator as well. To even things up, he had generously offered the job of narrator to Jamie, but she refused. "I'd rather you do it," she'd said. "You do it lots better than I ever could. I'll just read Guinevere's part."

Gavin the ham and Gavin the charitable battled it out. "But I'll have three parts and you'll have only one. That's not fair."

Jamie said, "I hate getting up in front of the class and you like it, so that makes it fair."

"Well, if you put it that way—Are you really sure?"

"Positive."

"Okay, then. But just remember, I offered."

Like a tireless taskmaster he had coached Jamie in her lines. "Slow down, slow down," he yelled when she read too fast. When the script called for her to give a scornful laugh and Jamie went, "Ha!" he said, "That's supposed to be a scornful laugh? Sounds more like a hiccup."

"And you sound like you think you're some Hollywood director."

"Look, Jamie, if we're going to do this, let's do it right. I want us to be better than anybody else in that class. To do that, you've just got to take it seriously. If I put everything I've got into it and you just yawn through, all it's going to do is make me look silly."

Jamie had to admit there was some truth in what he said. "Okay, Steven Spielberg, I'll take it seriously. Tell me how I should do it."

Gavin seemed to have a sense of perfect timing and phrasing. He read the lines to her as he wanted them spoken, then made her repeat them until he was satisfied that she was delivering them properly.

Now as they read before the class, she appreciated his careful coaching. She could tell that everyone was listening attentively, which made her even more diligent about expressing every line just the way Gavin had shown her. She could hear his voice in the back of her mind, still instructing. *Sound sad. Smile bitterly. Put a question mark in your voice.*

When they finally finished their scene, their classmates, who had so recently agonized over writing their own material, clapped approvingly. Even Ms. Schuyler clapped, Jamie noticed. She felt happy and embarrassed at the same time.

Gavin whispered in her ear, "We were sensational."

Ms. Schuyler said, "You two did a beautiful job, both in writing the scene and in reading it. Sounds as though you put in a lot of work. It was simply terrific." She turned to the class. "Now let's see how the rest of you measure up."

Jamie and Gavin took their seats, and the next paired couple began to read. Jamie's head was swimming. She knew she had Gavin to thank for her performance. He had helped her to impress Ms. Schuyler once again, and she was grateful to him for that. In fact, she was feeling kinder toward him than she had ever felt before. Although she had trouble concentrating on the rest of the readings, she could tell that none of the other students had put in as much work as she and Gavin had. For the most part, they read their lines without expression.

When the last pair finished, Ms. Schuyler said, "I'm proud of all of you. You've done a very nice job. Some things can still use simplifying and smoothing out. Leave your papers with me, and I'll look them over tonight to see how we can put them together." At that point the bell rang. Ms. Schuyler said, "Oh, Jamie and Gavin, will you both stay for a few minutes?"

"Sure," Gavin said.

As the other students filed out, Ms. Schuyler perched on a desk near Jamie, and Gavin joined them. "You two have done such a first-rate job of adapting 'Lancelot and Elaine' that I wondered how you'd feel about staying after school a few nights and helping me piece together the work of the others."

Gavin and Jamie exchanged surprised glances. Then Gavin shrugged and said, "It's okay with me."

"Me, too," Jamie said, delighted at any chance to be near her favorite teacher.

"Good. It shouldn't take too long to put it all together. Then I'd like a few of the students to give a reading for one of my other classes. I'm assigning them the 'Gareth and Lynette' story. This will give them an idea of how to go about dramatizing the material."

Gavin the blackmailer spoke up. "If we have to do all the work, then I think we should have our pick of the parts."

Ms. Schuyler smiled. "Fair enough."

"I take Lancelot," he said.

"Good. You'll make a wonderful Lancelot." She turned to Jamie. "And which part would you like to read, Cassandra-Jamie? Guinevere?" When Jamie hesitated, she added, "I do think, though, that you'd make an awfully good Elaine. How about it?"

Elaine the fair, Elaine the loveable,
Elaine, the lily maid of Astolat

"I wouldn't mind trying Elaine," Jamie said timidly. Imagine, Ms. Schuyler was giving her the very best role in the whole sketch! She must really like me, Jamie thought.

"Good. That's settled. I'll go over all the papers tonight

and grade them as they stand. Then tomorrow after school we'll get started on putting them together. And, oh yes, of course you'll get credit for the extra work."

Gavin walked part way with Jamie to her next class. "We'll rehearse together," he said. "When we're ready, we'll give Agnes a private performance."

Although Jamie realized that she could very definitely use Gavin's help, she resented his taking over so readily. "We'll see," she said.

"Hey, what was that Cassandra-Jamie business all about?"

Jamie took a Queen Guinevere pose. "Cassandra just happens to be my first name—my real first name."

"No kidding?"

"No kidding."

"I never knew that."

"There are many things you don't know about me, Gavin."

Gavin ignored Her Royal Highness. "How come if that's your real name you don't use it?"

In her you-are-really-being-very-tiresome voice, she said, "It's a long story and one I don't care to go into."

They had come to the spot where their paths parted. Gavin shook his head and said sarcastically, "Elaine the loveable."

❋   ❋   ❋

100

When Jamie returned home from school that afternoon, the first thing she said to Agnes was, "I think you and Daddy should start calling me Cassandra from now on. After all, it is my name."

❧ 12 ❧

Dear Ms. Schuyler

Dear Ms. Schuyler,

I think you are the most wonderful teacher in the whole world. You have made English my favorite subject this year, and I bet all your pupils feel the same way.

I have to tell you that you really bring out the best in people. There's this one boy I know who was always a pain to everybody—and I mean a lot of teachers, too. Since he's been in your class, he's getting much better. You just seem to know how to handle him and bring out his best. And, in my opinion, that is a super teacher who can do that.

You are also a beautiful person. I just love everything about you. I never told you this, but you remind me so much of my mother. She was a beautiful person, too.

I just think it would be so neat to have a special friend like you. The other kids wouldn't have to know if you didn't want them to. We could talk on the telephone and write each other notes and share our ideas about life. And we could call each other by our first names, Alex and Cassandra. Don't they sound great together when you say them that way?

Please be my special friend, Ms. Schuyler.

Hopefully,
Your Admirer,
Cassandra J. Cole

✤ 13 ✤

The Lily Maid
and the Noble Lord

For three days after school, Jamie and Gavin worked with Ms. Schuyler, turning the scenes the class had written into a solid play. Jamie had so much fun she wished the job could have lasted longer. Her only regret was that she couldn't have the teacher to herself.

When they finished, Ms. Schuyler had the script typed, then gave photo copies to the students she'd chosen to participate in the reading. "Practice your roles," she told them, "and on Wednesday after school we'll run through them before you make your formal presentation."

At home, Jamie said to Agnes, "Gavin's going to be Lancelot and I'm going to be Elaine. Ms. Schuyler said she thought I'd make an awfully good one. You know, Agnes, she's given us the best roles in the whole play."

"And why not, I'd like to know. Nobody's worked harder on that thing than you two."

"Oh, it's a wonderful role, Agnes. Elaine falls desperately in love with Lancelot. She says, 'Vain, in vain: it cannot be./He will not love me: how then? Must I die?'

All night long she keeps saying to herself, 'Must I die?' and 'Him or death. Death or him. Him or death.' It's very dramatic."

"Very," Agnes said.

"And then, when Lancelot gets better—you see, he'd been injured in this joust—Elaine tells him of her love. She says passionately, 'I have gone mad. I love you: let me die.'"

"And what does Lancelot say?"

"He tells her that he is three times her age and that she really isn't in love with him. What she feels for him, he says, is love's first flash in youth."

"Only a crush, huh?"

"That's what he means, but of course he doesn't say it that way. They didn't talk like that then."

"So he turns her down."

"Yes. He just doesn't understand. And she feels so indescribably desolate she makes up a song that starts off 'Sweet is pure love tho' given in vain, in vain,/ And sweet is death who puts an end to pain.'"

"That *is* sad," Agnes said.

"The only thing is I wish somebody besides Gavin was Lancelot." She thought about it for a moment, then added, "But maybe it's better this way. I mean, Gavin takes plays so seriously I can say stuff like, 'I have gone mad,' without feeling dumb. It would probably be worse with somebody else."

"You're absolutely right. It's bad enough to go mad without feeling dumb, too."

Jamie knew Agnes wasn't taking her seriously, but she didn't care. Talking to Agnes was a good way of getting her own thoughts together. She adored the idea of playing the lily maid of Astolat and just had to tell someone about it.

"I have gone mad. I love you; let me die," Jamie said as she and Gavin practiced their roles in her family room.

"Oh, boy," Gavin said. "Even a piece of frozen asparagus could show more feeling than that."

"Well, I don't care. I feel foolish. I'm afraid everyone will laugh."

"They sure will if you say it that way. Look, this far along in the play the people watching should be all caught up in the story. They already know what Elaine's going to say."

"What if they're not all caught up in the story?"

"They will be if we do it right. Besides, didn't you hear what Schuyler said? The class we're reading to is going to have to do the same thing with 'Gareth and Lynette.' We'll have a captive audience that's got to be receptive."

"But what if somebody laughs?"

"We're pros. We ignore it. Look, just pretend you're in love with this older guy. You want to tell him, and you're afraid to tell him. Just let the words 'I have gone mad,'

tumble out, then take a long pause and say, 'I love you,'
then pause again, and almost whisper, 'Let me die.' It'll
work that way."

Jamie sighed, then followed Gavin's instructions. She
had to admit the words *did* sound better that way. After
that, they worked all afternoon. When Elaine was in a
scene and Lancelot was not, Gavin read the other parts
so Jamie could practice her lines. She did the same for
him. Finally, exhausted, Jamie said, "I've had it. I'm beat
and I feel all cross-eyed."

"I was just getting into my stride," Gavin said.

"Oh, you—you never get tired."

"What do you mean? I'm always tired. Why, I don't
even walk in my sleep—I hitchhike."

"Oh, please, no jokes. I'm too worn out to do anything
that takes as much energy as laughing."

"Okay, lily maid—or should I call you Cassandra?"

"No. Not yet, anyhow."

"What do you mean, not yet?"

"I mean, I want to be called Cassandra, but not yet. I
talked to Agnes about it, and I guess she's right. She says
it would be better to wait until high school. Then there'll
be a lot of new kids who've never known me as Jamie.
It'll be easier for them to call me Cassandra. Nobody
would have to unlearn my name."

Gavin shrugged. "Suit yourself. You know, if you're
beat, I'm famished. Remember, all you've had to do is lie

on a barge and float dead down the river while I've been jousting—wounded even. Let's go see if Agnes has a quaff of ale for the battle-weary Lancelot."

The lily maid and the noble lord joined Agnes in the kitchen for homemade apple cake and milk. As they ate, Agnes said, "Whatever happened to all that fudge making, Gavin?"

He stared at her blankly for a second, then said, "Operations temporarily suspended, Lady Agnes. Who has time for culinary pleasures with all this rehearsing we have to do? The show must go on, you know."

As he and Agnes talked about the play, Jamie studied Gavin. He was thirteen, about eight months older than she, yet she had always thought of him as younger, probably because he was always so full of silly pranks. Somehow though, he seemed to have matured a little this semester. For the first time she realized that he wasn't bad-looking. He had the bluest eyes of anyone she knew, and his wavy sand-colored hair always looked neat. The sprinkle of freckles over his nose seemed to go with his impish smile. No, he definitely wasn't bad-looking at all. She hoped now that luck would make him her dancing partner, or that he would choose her for one of the free-choice numbers next week at Cotillion. He danced better than any of the other boys, and she wanted to appear at her best in front of Ms. Schuyler and her dad.

❊ ❊ ❊

The actors were as ready as they'd ever be to give a reading of "Lancelot and Elaine" to Ms. Schuyler's last period. They all had practiced together, but now that the moment had arrived, Jamie felt edgy. This was Wednesday, and Cotillion was only two days away. All that happening in one week seemed almost too much for Jamie.

As they were about to enter the classroom for their command performance, Gavin said to Jamie, "How y'doin'?"

She suspected that he could see how tightly wound up she was. "I'm so nervous my knees are knocking."

He deepened his voice in an imitation of some old-time movie director and said, "Just remember, Cole, you're going out there an unknown, but you're coming back a star!"

Jamie giggled and was relieved to find her tension lessening.

Ms. Schuyler introduced them all to their audience, then said to her last period, "I want you to listen very carefully, class. You'll be doing the same thing with another of the chapters from *Idylls of the King*. This will give you some idea of how to go about it."

The actors did, indeed, have a captive audience. There were a few early titters as the narrator set the scene, but from then on, the kids were attentive. Either they were caught up in the story, as Gavin had said they should be if it was performed properly, or they were listening intently, trying to figure out how to do their own assignment. Jamie couldn't decide which. At any rate, she felt they gave a creditable reading, and if the applause afterward wasn't deafening, it was at least respectable.

The last bell sounded soon after they finished. Ms. Schuyler asked them all to stay a few moments. "You should be very proud of the job you've done," she told them. They all modestly thanked her, and when they started to leave, she called back Jamie and Gavin.

"You two are just incredible," she said. "This is the kind of thing that's all too easy to ham up—especially the role of Elaine—but neither of you overacted. You read your parts just beautifully. If this were the Olympics, I'd rate you both 'ten.' As it is, you'll have to settle for an A."

Gavin said, "I'll bet you tell that to everyone who's brilliant."

Ms. Schuyler laughed good-naturedly and said, "Go on, get out of here. That's enough praise for one day."

The others had waited in the hall for Jamie and Gavin. Josh Hayden, who had been narrator and who had enunciated beautifully every word in the text, said, "Hey, we're gonna get a Coke or somethin'—you wanna go?"

Gavin said, "Sure."

Jamie, still glowing from the warmth of Ms. Schuyler's praise, felt waves of affection for this very select band of thespians and was flattered to be included. "Love to," she said.

They settled on the Frozen Yogurt Shop, about a block from school. There were nine of them, five boys and four girls, too many for one small table, so, with much chair scraping, they pushed together three tables. After they went through all the *What are you having?* and finally ordered, Trudy Kirsch, who played Guinevere, said, "You know, it's too bad we don't get to put on real plays in this school. I mean, on stage with costumes and everything."

Josh said, "Yeah, Trudy's right. There oughta be something like that."

"Yeah," Gavin said. "The Glee Club puts on operettas. How come there isn't some kind of acting club?"

Jamie sat listening to them argue the merits of a dramatic club, feeling the way she supposed people must feel when they're popular or a part of the "in" crowd.

Gavin said, "It's too late to get something like that going this year, but we could start them thinking about it for next year. Maybe we could even get Schuyler to take it on."

"That's a wonderful idea," Jamie said.

Gavin grinned. "I thought so, too."

Trudy said, "Well, if anything comes of it, let's pick plays that have more women's roles than this one did." She glanced at the two girls who'd had to read male parts.

"You can say that again," one of them said.

As she listened, Jamie's mind hopped ahead to Friday night. Cotillion. This just might be the happiest week of my whole life, she thought.

❧ 14 ❧
Cotillion

"Wear jeans, Daddy," Jamie told her father before he dressed for Cotillion.

"Jamie, you told me to wear jeans the last time I visited your school. Everybody else had on jackets and ties."

"That was different. Tonight we're having an Old West night, so everyone will be dressed in western-type clothes." Jamie had been ready for ages. She had on a blue-flowered calico dress with a ruffled peplum that she and Agnes had found in a Wild West store. Agnes had also plaited Jamie's dark hair to hang in one heavy braid down her back.

"Costume party, eh?" her father said, examining her outfit.

"Yes, Daddy."

"Maybe I should wear my spurs then."

"I didn't know you had spurs."

"I don't. That was a joke."

"Not funny," Jamie said. "And, Daddy, wear that plaid

shirt you wore when we went to your company's picnic last year."

"That old thing?"

"It looks western."

"Okay, okay. Maybe I should rent a horse for the occasion, too."

Jamie smiled tolerantly at his attempt at humor and said, "That's a good idea, but there just isn't enough time. And hurry up, or we'll be late."

When he was finally ready, Jamie made him tie one of her scarves around his neck. "Now you look more cowboyish," she said.

"I feel like a darned fool."

"Oh, Daddy, you look wonderful—really."

He sighed. "If you say so."

In the car, on the way to school, Jamie said, "I just know you'll love Ms. Schuyler. Everyone does. And this time, take a good look at her, Daddy, and you'll see how much she looks like Mother."

"Jamie, I've seen her, and except for the blond hair, she *doesn't* look like your mother."

Jamie said nothing, certain he would change his mind after tonight.

When they arrived at school, a little late, Jamie led him to the multi-purpose room, which was decorated with bales of hay. She spotted Ms. Schuyler in the corner of the room at the punch table, which was covered with a bandana-print tablecloth. "Come on, Daddy," Jamie said and led him through the groups of kids that were filtering in. When they reached the table, Ms. Schuyler flashed them her wide smile.

Jamie said, "You've already met my dad. He's going to chaperone with you tonight."

"Hi, Mr. Cole," Ms. Schuyler said.

"Rick," he said. "Can I be of help, Ms. Schuyler?"

"Alex. And, yes," she pointed to several white bakery boxes, "you can put the cookies on plates while I finish throwing some punch together."

"Sure thing."

They were off to a good start, Jamie thought. Alex and Rick. She noticed Trudy Kirsch and Debbie Michaels across the room and said, "I'll see you later, Daddy." He waved her off.

Usually she felt she was intruding when Debbie and Trudy were together, but at Cotillion the situation was different. Everyone seemed to feel that if they didn't have a bunch of people around them they might be considered wallflowers.

Debbie, a pretty redhead, said to Jamie, "I didn't know your dad was chaperoning tonight. I still think he's sexy-looking."

Trudy and Debbie were always saying that. Jamie glanced over at him. He was putting cookies on plates, which didn't look at all sexy to her. At the same time, she saw Gavin talking to Ms. Schuyler and wondered if he was asking her to take on a dramatic club next year.

Trudy said, "I really dig older men. I think I'll marry one. My grandmother always says, 'It's better to be an old man's darling than a young man's slave.'"

She and Debbie giggled. Jamie thought they sounded dumb, but she smiled anyhow.

At that point their instructor, who used only one name, Danielle, took her place in the middle of the polished floor and clapped her hands for attention. "Boys and girls, take your seats." She pointed to the chairs that lined the wall behind her. "Boys on this side." She nodded toward the chairs on the opposite wall. "Girls over there."

She was a tall, dramatic-looking woman. Tonight she wore jeans with high heels and a red silk shirt. Big silver hoops dangled from her ears. Jamie didn't think she looked very western, but no one seemed to care.

When everyone was seated, Danielle said, "Tonight, in keeping with our theme, we're going to learn the Texas Two-step. I know you'll find it a lot of fun."

As Danielle demonstrated, Jamie spotted Gavin across the room. She had only glimpsed him from the back when he was talking to Ms. Schuyler. Now she saw he was wearing boots, jeans, and a fancy, beaded western shirt that his grandparents had sent him as a gift when they retired in Arizona. He looked nice, she thought.

115

When Danielle finished showing them the steps, she enlisted the aid of her handsome teenage son, who often came with her and filled in as a partner for one of the girls if they needed an extra boy, as they often did. He partnered his mother in another demonstration of the Texas Two-step.

After that, Danielle said, "We're going to try something different tonight, boys and girls. I want all the girls to come over here to me." When no one moved, she added, "Come on now," and motioned them toward her. With suspicious looks on their faces, the girls slowly made their way to her side.

"Now I want you to take off your right shoe and put it here." She pointed to a spot on the floor. When the shoes formed a small pile, she said, "Now you can take your seats." They all limped back to their places.

Danielle turned to the boys. "When I say, 'Go,' I want you all to make a dash over to the shoes and grab one just as fast as you can. Then I want you to go find its owner. The girl wearing it will be your partner to start the Texas Two-step."

There was a lot of sniggering, and when Danielle said *Go*, the boys, looking embarrassed, sauntered rather than dashed over to the shoe pile. Danielle prodded them on with, "Quick, quick. Grab. Any shoe. Come on now!"

Jamie, fearful of who she would get for a partner,

wished now that Gavin had seen her, but she didn't think he had. He might have noticed that she was wearing black shoes with her white stockings. To her dismay, when all the boys had finally found their shoe-mates, she wound up with a partner who was half-a-head shorter than she. Of course she couldn't refuse to dance with him. That was against the rules.

Danielle put a cassette in the tape deck of the portable stereo, and soon lively music swept through the room. As Jamie tried out the new steps with her short partner, she glanced around until she found Gavin. He was dancing with a girl with long, blond hair, someone Jamie had never seen at Cotillion before. Nor could she remember seeing the girl around school.

As usual, Gavin had caught on to the new dance immediately, which was more than she could say for her partner. As they gamboled around the room, Gavin and the blond looked as though they were thoroughly enjoying themselves. Jamie tried to pretend she was having a good time, although she could hardly wait for the number to end. Her partner spent more time on *her* feet than on his own.

The music stopped abruptly, and they all had to change partners with the couples to their right. This time Jamie wound up with Josh Hayden, who turned out to be a better partner. The Texas Two-step started to take on some of the fun that Danielle had promised. To make matters even better, Josh told her what a great Elaine she had been. Then, of course, she told him that he was a sensational narrator. The evening was starting to move along nicely.

When Danielle was apparently satisfied that everyone was Texas Two-stepping properly, she changed the music so that they could all practice some of the dances they'd learned earlier: first, a polka; then, a waltz, one of the dances for which they were allowed to choose partners. Gavin usually chose Jamie, so she was fully expecting him to do so now. Instead, Josh asked her to dance. She hesitated for just a second, until she spied Gavin making his way onto the dance floor with the blond girl he had danced with earlier. Jamie graciously accepted Josh. After all, some people just didn't deserve the honor of a dance with the lily maid of Astolat.

When they were waltzing, to her great surprise she spotted her father dancing with Ms. Schuyler. She had no idea that her father could dance. And, oh, how embarrassed she would be if he was really bad. She was so worried, she almost lost her balance trying to watch him. To her amazement he was quite good, whirling Ms. Schuyler around and around gracefully.

Jamie was so concerned about his dancing ability that a few moments passed before the thought occurred to her that they were in each other's arms, her father and Ms.

Schuyler! At last he must have noticed the resemblance to her mother.

After that, Jamie felt as if she were moving around in a dream. When the waltz ended, Danielle told them all to take a break. Almost everyone made for the punch bowl.

Josh said to Jamie, "I'm gonna get something to drink. You coming?"

"I'll get something later," Jamie said and made no move to join him.

He excused himself and hurried toward the refreshment table. Although Jamie was dying to have words with her father, she knew that would be impossible until they were on their way home. Right now, he was being helpful, ladling out punch for a lineup of kids.

Jamie headed for the girls' room, which was already crowded. By the time she returned, the punch bowl was almost empty, but her dad managed to fill a cup for her. "You're late, Jamie. There was a big grab for the cookies, but I saved you one." He handed her a napkin-covered paper plate.

Before she accepted it, she glanced around, afraid someone might think her dad was giving her special treatment. No one seemed to be paying attention, however, not even Ms. Schuyler, who was tidying up the long table. As Jamie took the plate, he said, "Having a good time?"

"Oh, super," she said, exaggerating. "How about you?"

"It's an experience," he said noncommittally but with a twinkle in his eye.

Jamie wished she could have asked him about Ms. Schuyler, but she realized this was neither the time nor the place. Instead, she took her refreshments and joined Trudy and Debbie until Danielle was ready to begin again.

As the dance instruction continued, Jamie kept glancing over at her dad and Ms. Schuyler, gratified to find them often deep in conversation. When the next number came along, where they were all allowed to choose partners, Jamie looked around until she spotted Gavin. She fully expected to find him headed for the blond girl. Instead, he was whispering something to Josh. Jamie saw Josh nod, then make his way through the crowd. Gavin headed straight for Jamie.

"This one's going to be a rumba," he said. "How about it?"

"Okay," Jamie said. She noticed Josh across the room, talking to the blond. Gavin apparently had asked him to dance with her. She must be a visiting relative of Gavin's, Jamie decided, no longer feeling rejected. Naturally he'd have to pay attention to a relative, if only to be polite.

When the music started and they began dancing, Jamie said, "Did you ask Ms. Schuyler about starting a dramatic club next year?"

"She won't be here next year."

Jamie, stunned, stopped dancing.

"Hey, what did I do—step on your toes or something?"

She pulled herself together. "No, nothing like that. I was just surprised, that's all. How do you know she's not going to be here?"

They began dancing again, and he said, "I came early to ask her about the club. She said that even though she couldn't put one together, she thought the idea was a good one. She's going to talk to the vice-principal about it."

Jamie, no longer interested in the club, said, "If she's not going to be here, where *is* she going to be?"

"Some college near Los Angeles."

Oh, no, Jamie thought, unwilling to abandon her wonderful dream. Her dad would just have to work awfully fast. The school year was almost over. Ms. Schuyler would probably soon be heading back to San Francisco for the summer. That was where she'd said her family lived. Jamie couldn't quite deal with the idea of her favorite teacher disappearing from her world. There had to be a way to stop her, and Jamie was sure she would find it. For the moment, she tried to turn her thoughts to less serious subjects. "Who was that blond girl you were dancing with for the free-choice number?"

"You mean you haven't met her?"

"No. Why should I have?"

"Schuyler introduced a bunch of us to her when we first came in."

"I was late."

"Schuyler said she didn't know anybody. She asked me to dance with her and help her get acquainted."

"I thought she was a relative of yours."

"Mine! Didn't you know? She's Ms. Schuyler's daughter."

If the news that Ms. Schuyler was leaving came as a bombshell to Jamie, Gavin's new information had the wallop of a nuclear blast.

Gavin went on talking. "I guess Schuyler must be divorced. Mia's been staying with her grandparents in San Francisco. She's just down for the weekend. She says that next term her mother's going to take an apartment near the college where she'll be working, and they'll be together again."

Mia. The girl with the long, blond hair, the girl Gavin had danced with when he should have been dancing with Jamie, was Ms. Schuyler's daughter! The words she'd written in the letter she'd never had the courage to send came back to her now, and she felt as ashamed and humiliated as if she *had* sent the letter. *Please be my special friend.* Ms. Schuyler already had her own special friend, her daughter. She certainly didn't need Jamie.

Jamie fought back tears. Disappointment felt like a

hard lump in her throat that just wouldn't go down. There were times, though, when you had to pretend you were having a good time, even if you were dying inside.

In the car on the way home, Jamie's father said, "You seem very quiet."

"I'm just tired," Jamie said.

"Me, too. By the way, your favorite teacher seems to be leaving the school. Did you know?"

"I heard. And she's not my favorite teacher."

"Oh? I thought she was."

Jamie, swallowing hard, said, "No."

"You never mentioned that she had a daughter."

"I didn't know."

"Oh, really? Did you have a chance to meet her tonight?"

"No."

"She seems like a nice kid."

Jamie said nothing for a long time, then finally blurted out, "Are you going to ask Sylvia Dennis to marry you?"

He said, "I already did."

Although she'd had two shocks that evening, she was not prepared for another. She took a moment to take in the words, then said, "Oh, Daddy, how could you?"

"Don't get excited. She turned me down."

That was an even greater jolt to Jamie. "Why?" she asked, not believing her ears.

123

He chuckled. "I suspect she doesn't want to take on the rearing of a difficult adolescent."

Jamie bristled. "I'm not difficult."

"I'm kidding, Jamie. That's not the reason. The truth is, she had a bad marriage and she just isn't quite ready to try again. At least, not right now anyhow. Maybe someday she'll change her mind. And talking of Sylvia, I just found out last night that she went to Vassar, and very close to the time your mother was there. Small world, I guess."

Vassar, the college Jamie wanted to go to, the college that Agnes always said turned out independent women, the kind of women who could go out into the community and do what needed to be done. Sylvia surely wasn't one of those. Of course, she had never graduated. The night that Jamie and her dad had dinner with her, she'd said that she had only completed three years. That probably made a difference. "How come she didn't tell you until now?"

"Good question. I don't know. Somehow we never got around to talking about our school days. I guess it just didn't seem important."

Jamie had to think about that, along with Sylvia's strange reaction to her father's proposal. In fact, she had to think about this whole evening. None of it had turned out the way she had expected.

⚜ 15 ⚜

Cassandra Alone

Cassandra, alone, strolls through the gardens at Versailles, conscious as she passes that heads are turning to stare at her. The curious. Some of their whispers reach her ears.

"Who is the beautiful stranger who carries herself as proudly as Marie Antoinette, who once walked these very paths?"

"No one knows. She is a mystery. But see how sadly she smiles. There must be great pain in her heart."

They cannot know that in another time, another happier time, she had visited this same spot, smelled the perfume of these same flowers. There was laughter then, and joy. Now there is only sadness, the sadness of the wronged.

Now Cassandra cannot go on to France, to Rome to see the glorious promised wonders. Nor can she stay up until the wee hours talking and talking, for there is no one with whom to talk. There is only Cassandra. Alone.

❦ 16 ❦

A Spiffy Idea

On the Wednesday following Cotillion, Jamie came home from school through a fine, dreary mist that matched the mood that had hung over her since Friday night.

Agnes, as usual, was working in the kitchen. "I wish it would rain and get it over with," she said. When she received no response from Jamie, she added, "Well, how was your day?"

"Okay," Jamie said.

Agnes said, "Cookies in the cookie jar. I made them this morning. Help yourself, Jamie. I want to get this casserole ready so you and your daddy can just slip it into the oven tonight. Hector and I are going to an early movie."

Jamie automatically moved toward the cookie jar, then stopped abruptly. "I'm not hungry, Agnes. Thanks anyhow."

Agnes stopped what she was doing and, with a worried expression, looked at Jamie. "What's the matter with you,

Jamie? You've been mooning around here for days now and eating like a bird. You aren't sick, are you?"

"No, I'm okay. It's just that I've had a lot on my mind." Jamie took a seat at the table and helped herself to a black jelly bean, which she studied as carefully as if it held the secret to the universe.

"A lot on your mind, huh? Like what?"

"I mean, I had a lot of thinking to do about a lot of things." She popped the jelly bean into her mouth and sucked on it.

"Well, did you get it done—all that thinking?"

"Some." In truth, Jamie had acted first and thought afterward. On Saturday morning she'd snatched her carefully guarded letter from its hiding place, the letter she'd meant to send when things had worked out to her satisfaction. Then she borrowed one of Agnes's kitchen matches and a clay saucer from one of the geranium plants in the backyard. In the wooded area behind her house, she tore the letter into many small pieces, then set them aflame in the saucer and watched them burn to ash. When the ash was cool to the touch, she held up the saucer and blew the remains into the wind, which carried them away. The ritual was symbolic of a beautiful dream that was never to be.

Beautiful? No, silly was more like it. Stupid was even closer to the truth. After that, she started thinking.

Agnes said now, "Well, with all that thinking, did you come to any conclusions?"

"Some."

"Care to share them?"

Jamie helped herself to a pink jelly bean and studied it as intently as she had the black one. "Well, for one thing I've changed my mind about Elaine."

Agnes looked blank. "Elaine?"

"You know—Elaine and Lancelot."

"Oh, *that* Elaine, the one who died for love. I thought you liked that role."

"Oh, I did—as a role. But, at first, I thought what she did was romantic."

"And now?"

"Now I think it was really dumb."

"Oh?"

"Yes. I mean, Lancelot had a whole other life that she couldn't know anything about. Elaine didn't know him at all, so she was pretty silly to think she was in love with him. Besides, he was in love with Guinevere. If Elaine had known that, I bet she would have felt really stupid doing what she did."

"I'd like to think you're right."

"I know I'm right," Jamie said defensively. "She was silly and stupid."

"Well, that's certainly clear thinking, I'd say." Agnes

went back to preparing the casserole. "Come up with anything else?"

"Not really. But I've been doing a lot of thinking about my father and Sylvia Dennis. Did you know that he asked her to marry him?"

Agnes stopped her work again. "So that's what you've been stewing about."

"I haven't been stewing. I've been thinking."

"And when is all this supposed to take place?"

"It isn't. She said no. Can you imagine that?"

"No, I can't. Your father is an attractive man. Plenty of women would jump at the chance."

"That's what I think."

"Did she say why?"

Jamie passed on the reason her father had told her. When Agnes raised her eyebrows, Jamie added, "And you know what else, Agnes? She went to Vassar, the same college my mother went to and at almost the same time."

Agnes said, "Well, remember what I always told you, Vassar women are very independent."

"But don't you think it's strange? I mean, it seems almost too much to be a coincidence. And something else they have in common—they both gave up smoking."

"Lots of people went to Vassar. That's not exactly what I'd call a coincidence. As for smoking, everybody's giving it up."

"All the same, it seems strange." Jamie licked the pink jelly bean. "You know something, Agnes? My mother always used to say that she never really learned anything at Vassar except the most important thing—where to find out what she had to know. I was never quite sure what that meant. I'm still not."

"Maybe you should ask Sylvia. She went to Vassar. She ought to know."

"Oh, I couldn't do that."

"Why not?"

"Well, I don't really know her. I mean, just meeting someone a couple of times doesn't mean you really know her. Especially someone like Sylvia."

"I thought you knew her well enough to know you didn't like her."

"No, Agnes, you're wrong. It's because I didn't know her that I thought I didn't like her. I can't really tell whether I like her or not, because I still don't know her."

Agnes peered at her quizzically. "I have the feeling that must make some kind of sense. I just haven't figured out what it is."

Jamie ignored her. "I think it would take a long time to get to know someone like Sylvia."

"That deep, is she?"

"Well, you can tell that she must have suffered. I mean, with a bad marriage and a little boy who was killed. You have to lose someone yourself before you can understand something like that. And, don't forget, she *did* go to Vassar, even though she didn't graduate."

"And, what's more, she turned down your father. A very complex woman, I'd say."

"I think you're right, Agnes. It's my opinion that first impressions are usually way off. You can't really tell anything about people until you know them better."

"I'm glad you're finding that out," Agnes said. "Any further conclusions?"

"Yes. I've been thinking a lot about destiny, and I've decided I still believe in it. If bad things happen, it's only because something else good is coming up. I still truly believe that."

Before Agnes could respond, the back door opened and Gavin's head appeared as he said, "Knock, knock."

Agnes, as always, willingly played into his hands. "Who's there?" she asked.

"Isabelle," he said.

"Isabelle who?"

"Isabelle out of order? I had to knock."

"Terrible," Jamie said, shaking her head.

"Thank you," he said and held up his two-cup measure. "I'm back to the kitchen, Lady Agnes. I'll master the fine art of making fudge yet."

"You know where the canister is. Help yourself, Gavin." Agnes continued putting her casserole together.

"What are you making?" he asked.

"A recipe that came down from my dear grandmother. It's called Wednesday chicken—closely related to Sunday chicken."

"Sounds good." He measured out the sugar from the canister, then sat down at the table opposite Jamie and helped himself to a handful of jelly beans from the glass jar. "I sure hate this yukky weather. I wish it would rain."

"That's what Agnes just said."

"We always agree, don't we, Lady Agnes?"

"Always," Agnes said.

He threw one of his jelly beans into the air and, as it came down, caught it in his mouth. Then he said, "Only three more weeks of school."

"I know." Jamie could hardly wait until the term was over and Ms. Schuyler only a memory.

As if he had ESP, he said, "I'm really going to miss Schuyler. She's a good teacher. I learned a lot from her."

Jamie said indignantly, "She may be a good teacher, but I don't think it was very nice of her, not telling people that she had a daughter."

"So whose business was it anyhow? Besides, at least one of her other classes knew. When she introduced some of us to Mia at Cotillion, I heard this kid say, 'When she mentioned having a daughter, I pictured someone about six years old.' I guess the subject just didn't happen to come up with us."

132

"Humph," Jamie said, not willing to give Ms. Schuyler the benefit of the doubt.

Gavin, apparently aware of her hostility, said, "You know, we both have a lot to thank her for."

Jamie scowled. "What? I'd like to know."

"What? All right, I'll give you *what. What* is that she gave us both a chance to do something that we'd never done before. I mean, I really felt good, working on that play. I think you did, too. In fact, you'll have to admit we made a good team."

Jamie wasn't about to admit anything. She merely shrugged.

"Which reminds me, there's something I want to talk to you about."

"Oh? What?"

"Well, I've been thinking. We have a three-car garage, and one section is empty because my sister always parks outside. This summer a bunch of us could get together— you and me and Josh and Trudy and whoever else is interested. We could put on plays there."

"You mean, before an audience?"

"Sure."

"What audience?"

"Oh, there're always people who'll come to anything that's free."

As he went on talking about all the great one-acts he'd

133

been looking at in the library, Jamie thought, he's probably just the person who could really put something like that together and make it work. She remembered how good she'd felt, sharing Cokes that afternoon with the group she'd worked with on "Elaine and Lancelot," and how sorry she'd been to see the project come to an end.

She interrupted him. "Gavin, I don't mean to change the subject, but you're always saying that your fudge is no good. Why don't you make it here?"

He looked almost shocked. "Here?"

"Yes. I'll help, and Agnes can show us how. If you really want to learn, she's a good cook. And then you'll have a chance to tell me more about your play idea."

"Oh . . ." He glanced shyly over at Agnes who was now slipping the prepared casserole into the refrigerator. "What do you think, Lady Agnes?"

"I think that's a spiffy idea. I just happen to be the world's dandiest fudge-maker," Agnes said.

"Can't do better than that for a teacher," he said.

Jamie said, "And Agnes, before I forget, I really think we should think about having Sylvia to dinner some night."

Agnes, with raised eyebrows, turned to look at her. "Does that mean you want to get to know her better?"

"Of course not. It doesn't mean anything. But you know she had me to lunch. It's only polite to pay her back somehow."

"Oh, right. I'd forgotten about that," Agnes said solemnly, but a little smile played at the corners of her mouth.

Outside the day was misty and chilly. The kitchen, warm and cozy and soon to be full of the delicious fragrance of chocolate, was a good place to spend the afternoon.